TH

Michael Hardcas[tle]
in Yorkshire. Af[ter]
in the Royal Arm[y]
embarking on a career in journalism, work-
ing in a number of roles for provincial daily
newspapers from reporter to chief feature
writer.

He has written more than one hundred
children's books since his first was published
in 1966, but still finds time to visit schools
and colleges all over Britain to talk about
books and writing. In 1988 he was awarded
an MBE in recognition of his services to
children's books. He is married and lives in
Beverley, near Hull.

by the same author

The Fastest Bowler in the World

One Kick

Own Goal

Quake

Second Chance

Please Come Home

in the Goal Kings series

They All Count

Michael Hardcastle

Goal Kings
BOOK FOUR

faber and faber

First published in 1999
by Faber and Faber Limited
3 Queen Square London WC1N 3AU

Typeset by Avon Dataset, Bidford-on-Avon, Warwickshire
Printed and bound in England by Mackays of Chatham PLC,
Chatham, Kent

A CIP record for this book
is available from the British Library

ISBN 0–571–19366–8

2 4 6 8 10 9 7 5 3 1

Contents

1 Park Play

Danny Loxham was perched on the back of a wooden bench near the entrance to Candle Park, apparently studying the bound script of a play called *How Do They Know*? In fact, most of the time the captain and keeper of Rodale Goal Kings Football Club was keeping an eye on anyone who came into the park from any direction. Apart from being given one of the leading roles in next term's school play he'd had a poor day at school and was looking forward to a better evening. If a certain person turned up in the next few minutes the day would turn into a triumph.

Then, to his great surprise, someone pushed him so hard in the back he almost fell off the seat and he heard a gleeful whisper, 'Got you! You're losing concentration, skipper! The coach won't like that.'

Recovering his poise, Danny swung round

to face the tall, fair-haired figure of his team-mate Josh Rowley looking as pleased as if he'd scored a hat trick of headers. 'How'd you manage to creep up on me like that? I mean, I *was* completely lost in this play I'm reading but . . .'

'Just talent, that's all, Danny boy! The true instinct of a striker who ghosts into the box without anyone noticing his arrival.'

'Rubbish! You're a back-four defender. And defenders are supposed to help out their keeper, not knock 'em about.'

'Listen, dear Mrs Allenby knows I'm a striker at heart but at present she's just play-ing me in defence to learn a few tricks of the trade, striker's tricks, I mean. She always insists I go up for free kicks and corners 'cos I'm always likely to get a goal, aren't I?'

'Only because you're about ten miles taller than anybody else in the team. Anyway, what're you doing here, Josh? Never seen you in Candle Park at this time. You usually go straight home to get your homework done.'

'Don't have any tonight. Just happened to spot you and wondered why you're stuck here all on your own. I mean, if you're reading a book you don't have to do it in the middle of nowhere. Unless it's a *dirty* book. Hey, let's have a look –'

'Get your hands off! It's a play and I'm learning my lines. I prefer peace and quiet and that's why I'm here. I was getting it, too, until you turned up. Now –'

He stopped as someone hailed them in a familiar Scottish accent. 'Hey, you guys! What's going on here? You having a secret meeting or something?'

They turned to see Frazer McKinnon approaching, his schoolbag slung over his left shoulder, a tennis ball at his feet.

Danny ignored the questions and put one of his own: 'What is this? A defenders' union get-together? All I wanted was some peace and suddenly this place is as crowded as a penalty area for a corner kick. What are you after, Oats?'

Frazer, who never objected to his 'porridge' nickname, raised his eyebrows. 'I just saw you guys together and thought we might have a friendly kickabout. Didn't realize you were having a row. So –'

'A row? We're not having a row,' Josh

insisted. 'Why'd you say that, Oats?'

'Because Danny sounds angry, really mad at me for just being here. If that's how you feel I'll disappear.'

'No, listen –' Danny was starting to say when he caught sight of someone else approaching from beside the war memorial on the other side of the park. The other boys saw the intensity of his gaze and turned to see what had magnetized him.

'Isn't that Sophie Crosland? You know, the one who got picked for the county netball team?' remarked Frazer. 'She's in the same side as my sister.'

Josh, however, had seen beyond mere recognition. 'That's who you're waiting for, isn't it, Danny? You fancy her!'

Danny was going to admit nothing, though his cheeks now had a pinkish hue. 'Rubbish! Told you, I was just quietly sitting here, thinking about the part I've got in this new play and, er, well, how I should interpret the character. That's the way you've got to do it if the audience are going to believe in you. That's what Mrs Martens says and everybody knows she's the best drama teacher the school's ever had.'

Josh wasn't listening but he was aware that Danny had scarcely taken his eyes off the tall, chestnut-haired girl who had paused as if uncertain which way to go but now was briskly walking away in the opposite direction from them. Danny's eyes narrowed but his voice didn't falter. Josh sensed he'd summed up the situation with total accuracy.

'How long's it been going on, then, Dan?' he couldn't resist enquiring.

'*Nothing*'s going on, Josh, so forget it. I just talk to Sophie sometimes, that's all. I mean, she likes sport. So, well, we just talk – sometimes.'

Frazer had been thinking along different lines. 'Does she play soccer then, that lass?'

Danny, glad to escape from the tangle he'd been getting into, shook his head. 'Don't believe so. As Josh says, netball's her game. Oh, and tennis. She's pretty good at that.'

'My sister's crazy on soccer, can't get enough of it,' Frazer revealed. 'Thinks she might get into the Goal Kings' team one day. Over my dead body that'll be! I want to be in a team that wins things.'

Now that Sophie was out of sight Josh had

lost interest in her and was happy to return to their favourite topic of conversation. 'So what d'you think of this new idea of Mrs Allenby's?' he enquired. 'Bet there can't be many coaches who train their teams on a ploughed field!'

Danny, thankful to get away from the subject of Sophie, managed a laugh. 'It's not a *ploughed* field, Josh! It's a meadow. That means it'll be uneven and with sloping bits here and there. Might be good fun.'

'Oh, it's all right for you,' Oats pointed out. 'All you've got to do is catch the ball or belt it as far as you can. We've got to pass the ball along the ground. If we don't get it right she's bound to drop the worst performers. I've got to make sure I'm not one of them. Fact is I tried it out with my sister on a bumpy field near us. I tell you, it's not easy.'

'If it was easy Jane wouldn't be getting us to do a practice session like this,' Danny pointed out. 'Oh yes, Oats, and don't get the idea I have no problems with the state of the pitch. I have to look out for a bad bounce or a ball skidding through when it's greasy. If the ball hits a sort of lump – a divot, that's the word, isn't it? – well it could take off right over my head when I go down for it. I know, I've seen it happen even to an England keeper. On TV, I mean. So I'll be under pressure on this meadow pitch.'

As if to underline how seriously he was taking this he unwrapped a stick of his favourite chewing gum and popped it into his mouth, a routine he now practised at the start of every match in the Highlea Sunday League. Rodale Goal Kings had started the new season disappointingly and then things appeared to take a sharp turn for the worse with the resignation of their ambitious coach, Ricky Todd. In one sense, Ricky was almost following in the footsteps of his son, Alex, a talented striker, who earlier had walked out on the team after being dropped by his father because of poor form. Ricky had handed over his responsibilities to his assistant, the team's physio, Jane Allenby, whose own son, Dominic was one of the Kings' central defenders and a former winner of the player-of-the-season award. Jane, who worked as a midwife and thus had lots of medical knowledge, was showing great enthusiasm for her new coaching role and some of her innovations had surprised her team.

'Listen, where do you think the coach gets all her ideas from?' Frazer asked. 'I mean, she wasn't a player herself, was she? I know there's a lot of women's football about these days, even on the telly, but she never mentions that she played for anyone.'

Josh shrugged but then said, 'Maybe she just talks to other coaches and pinches their best ideas. Coaches are always yakking to each other when they meet, so maybe they have regular get-togethers in secret, swapping suggestions and stuff like that. Except, well, I'm sure Ricky wasn't like that. Never talked to anybody if he could help it, did he?'

Danny, back on his perch with his feet planted on the seat itself, was still casting yearning glances towards the path Sophie had taken. What he'd do if she suddenly reappeared he wasn't quite certain but he'd have to find some excuse to give to his team-mates so that he could dash off to talk to her. Meanwhile, he listened intently to their comments about coaches.

'She reads all Dominic's magazines, his football mags,' Danny revealed. 'That's what

Dom says, anyway. Even when he puts them in different places in his bedroom, you know, sort of hides them, his mum still finds them. Oh yes, and Dom says she spends an age chatting on the phone to other football people. So that confirms what you said, Oats.'

By now Frazer had tired of the talk and was bouncing his tennis ball from instep to knee and then trying to get it to his shoulder from where it could run down his back before being flicked upwards with his heel. That was a trick he managed quite often in private practice, and sometimes with his sister Andrea, but he failed to pull it off in public.

'Tell you one thing, though,' he added to cover up another slightly misjudged knee bounce, 'she thinks defenders are just as important as attackers. Old Ricky only cared about the forwards, probably because that's where Alex played. But Jane says if teams don't concede goals they don't lose matches.'

'Nobody's going to argue with that,' Danny agreed. 'But if teams don't *score* goals they don't win 'em, either. So a coach has got to think about the *whole* team. Oh, and so has the assistant coach *when* there is one.' He paused and then added: 'Of course, Mrs Allenby may want me to do that job.'

He said it with such an air of seriousness that his team-mates were quite sure he meant it. After all, at her first training session after taking over from Ricky Todd she had put Danny in charge of one group of players while she worked with the remainder. Since then Danny had come to believe that he really could be her choice if she decided to appoint a second-in-command.

'Listen, mate, you might not even have the captaincy if Foggy gets his way,' Josh pointed out. 'You know he's never given up the idea that he should be skipper. Thinks his foghorn voice entitles him to special favours. As if! But you know Fogs, never stops shouting about how good he is, does he? So Mrs Allenby may just give him the job to see if he can actually do it.'

Danny gave the towering defender a cool look. 'That's quite shrewd of you, Josh. Sure the coach hasn't been giving you some inside information, that she's planning a change, I mean?'

Josh grinned. 'You'll just have to wait and see, *captain*!'

'Aye, maybe she is, but she also fancies Reuben,' confided Frazer who was beginning to feel left out of the chat between team-mates who'd known each other a lot longer than they'd known him. Frazer's family had moved to the village of Rodale Kings from their native Scotland only the previous season and it had taken time to establish himself as a member of the Kings' squad. 'Reuben could easily be her favourite player. She says she's got definite plans for him.'

'Reuben!' Danny and Josh exclaimed simultaneously. Then Danny added, 'But Reuben's gone off. He's not half as good as he was when he played against us a couple of seasons ago for Stonecreek Pirates. I mean, Ricky was always shouting at him during matches. Said he wasn't putting in enough effort, that sort of thing. You couldn't have somebody like that, a non-trier, as skipper. No way!'

'Aye, but don't forget it was Mrs Allenby who got him to sign for us when he fell out with the Pirates,' Frazer said. 'That's maybe why Ricky didn't rate him because he didn't choose him. Thing is, Reuben told me that Mrs Allenby told him after training that she had real plans for him, she was going to build the team round him. How about that, you guys?'

Danny didn't know what to say so, sensibly, he said nothing. Yet he couldn't help wondering whether he might have to surrender the captaincy. It was one of Foggy's arguments that a captain had to be an outfield player because a goalkeeper was often too far from the action to know exactly what was going on. On the other hand, Danny believed that the captaincy was basically an honour and he'd earned it because of his skills and his consistently good performances as a keeper. He liked leading the team out, tossing up with rival captains and then doing his best to keep up his team's spirits. In his view Reuben was a bit like Foggy, far too concerned with his own play and feelings to think enough about team-mates.

'Tell you who will know, bound to – Dominic,' Josh said. 'Why don't we ask him at training tonight?'

Danny was shaking his head. 'Even if he

knows I don't think he'll tell us. Dominic's hardly speaking to anybody these days about anything. I think maybe his mum has warned him not to give away her plans when the team's all together, so he's doing as he's told. Pity.'

'Funny you should say that, Dan, because I have the idea that Dominic doesn't say much because he's just *listening* to us,' Josh remarked. 'Then anything he hears that he thinks his mum would like to know about, he tells her.'

'Hey, a spy in the dressing-room! Sounds like the title of a really good football book,' Frazer suggested.

'Oats, that's not fair!' Danny reproved him. 'Dom's not like that, he wouldn't *spy* on his own mates. I think he's just a bit embarrassed about his mum being the coach, that's all. I'm sure I'd feel the same if I were in his shoes. Doesn't mean I can't sympathize with Dom. It was different with Alex because he just tried to make the most of being Ricky's son. He used to say his dad would never drop *him* from the side so he could do what he liked. Then when Ricky did drop him Alex walked out, didn't he? Dom would never be like that.'

Josh was nodding. 'Yeah, I go along with that, Danny. Sorry I made him sound like a spy. He's a really good mate and I like playing alongside him, except when I get the chance to go forward and show the strikers how to score goals!'

'Listen, you guys, I've got things to do before training,' Oats announced. 'Might just get a chance to use Andrea as a target board again. Want to be on my best form because I think our season's going to take off from now on. See you later.'

Danny thought the Scottish boy might be a 'wee bit embarrassed', as he himself might put it, by his 'spy' remark but the skipper wasn't going to say so. Contentedly he watched him and Josh head out of the park, exchanging sharp passes with the tennis ball. Then, when they'd gone, Danny energetically leapt off his seat and raced away in the direction Sophie had taken. He guessed she'd be too far away by now for him to catch her up but it was definitely worth a try.

2 The Passing Game

'Don't know why this field is called Moore's Meadow,' remarked Davey Stroud as he stood at the top of the slope and looked down towards the distant river. 'It ought to be christened Moles' Meadow. Must be millions of 'em under there, judging by all those molehills.'

'Oh, I didn't know all those little piles of dirt were made by *moles*,' confessed Matthew Forrest innocently. 'Are you sure, Davey?'

'Of course I'm sure!' insisted Davey, his startlingly blue eyes wide in surprise at such a question. 'Honestly, Tree, I can't believe you didn't know that. *Everyone* can recognize a molehill. But I suppose defenders can never be as brilliant as strikers. That's why top clubs pay millions for goal-scorers.' He was going to add 'like me' but thought better of it.

Tree, fortunately, didn't feel insulted and continued to survey the uneven surface. He thought it would be impossible to control the ball if it bounced off any of the bumps on this thinly-grassed meadow. Why on earth had Jane Allenby chosen to practise on it?

A few minutes later the Rodale Kings' coach told him and the rest of the squad just what she had in mind. 'Sometimes soccer is called the passing game,' she began as they grouped round her by the wide swing gate that led into the meadow from a sunken lane flanked by hawthorn hedges. 'If you think about it, that's true. Just about everything depends on the quality and speed and accuracy of a pass from one player to another. Well, probably anybody who thinks he's a player can pass a ball a short distance with the side of his foot on a flat, really smooth surface. But what about a bumpy pitch with divots as big as boulders? Well, like tennis balls, anyway! How d'you cope with a pass that hits one of those and shoots off in any direction?'

Mrs Allenby, glancing round the faces of her players, looked for signs of boredom. She knew they really wanted only to get on with kicking a ball, however badly or well they did it. The last thing they wanted at the end of a school day was a lecture. To her, however, it was important to make them understand what she really needed from them if the Kings were to challenge for trophies. Enthusiasm, though many of them possessed an abundance of it, wasn't enough on its own. To her surprise, Danny was the only player who was looking distinctly fed up. But then, perhaps that was understandable because passing wasn't really a skill demanded of him.

The question she'd put didn't draw any answers because they already knew her well enough to realize she'd continue in a moment. So she did, speaking very slowly indeed, to emphasize the importance of the next few words. 'Well, it's how you cope with a *difficult* pass that sorts out the *top* players from the rest. If you can control the ball immediately after getting a bad bounce or when its spinning wildly then you're the player a top manager will always want. Don't forget that giving a good pass is just as vital as being able to receive one. Sorry to talk so much, Kings, but what I've just said to you is probably as important as anything I'm ever going to say to you in the future.'

'I know one thing that's even better, Coach,' said Lloyd Colmer with one of his infectious grins. 'You'll say, "Well done, Kings, you've won the Championship!" And we'll all agree with you!'

'Nice one, Lloyd,' agreed Danny.

'Yes, that'll be the best, Lloyd,' his coach acknowledged. 'And let's hope I'll be saying it this season. Not much chance, though, if we don't improve on recent results. We can't wait any longer to start winning. Tonight's training is linked to that ambition.'

She explained that the players would form a large oval and run in a clockwise direction with at least a couple of metres between players. In the centre of the oval would be Reuben Jones who would hit a pass to each player in turn and then receive the ball back from the same player. Anyone who failed to take his pass would have to retrieve the ball from wherever it finished up and then return it to Reuben from that point.

'That way you'll be passing the ball on the run and have to be ready for any awkward bounce it takes. No one can predict how it will bounce on this surface,' she concluded. 'OK, that's it, except to say that I'm giving Reuben the orange bib so you'll be able to pick him out wherever you are.'

'He doesn't need it,' Joe Parbold pointed out. 'Nobody could miss someone with hair that colour!'

Reuben was renowned almost as much for the shade of his hair, an astonishing silvery white, as the brilliance of his left foot. Jane saw him as the Kings' playmaker, operating from just behind the team's twin strikers and joining them in attack whenever possible. Reuben had never imagined that scoring goals might be part of his game. Until Jane Allenby had spotted his potential Reuben had been content to remain at the back of midfield.

'What about me, Coach?' enquired Danny, disappointed she hadn't given him a special role.

'Well, I want you to join in with everybody else, Danny. Goalkeepers usually claim they'd be brilliant outfield players, don't they? So –'

'I am! I was the one who scored the best goal ever when we won the Highlea Knock-out Cup. I took the ball the length of the pitch. Nobody could forget that!'

Jane nodded. 'True but now we need pin-point passes, Danny, not spectacular goals. If ever I need you to play in an outfield role then you must be as good with your feet as anybody else.'

As soon as the exercise began and the first passes were made it was all too plain how diabolical the surface was for football. The ball would sometimes shoot up vertically to the consternation of the receiver; and sometimes, on hitting a molehill, stop dead so that the would-be kicker simply over-ran it. Very few passes went exactly where intended and even the elegant and precise Reuben was fooled by the eccentric bounce.

Soon the players began to laugh at the bizarre incidents and that suited Jane because it showed they were enjoying themselves. Most of the time she simply watched, her silence allowing them to find their own ways of coping with such an unnatural surface. If training couldn't sometimes be sheer fun then it lost its value. That, anyway, was her philosophy, though she couldn't put it to her boys in quite those words in case they were tempted to tax her with it when they were tired or bored.

The biggest explosion of laughter came when Danny, in sheer exasperation at being unable to trap the ball, picked it up and hurled it under-arm at Reuben, mimicking the kind of clearance he sometimes made from his own goal area. Rather to Jane's surprise Reuben joined in the joke by flicking the ball upwards and then heading it to the player nearest to him, who happened to be Davey. Most of the time Reuben was rather solemn; he hardly ever joined in any of the fooling that was normal in a group of boys of his age. His coach discovered that was because he was the eldest of a large family and thus was expected to take extra responsibilities at home. 'That's why I'd never want to be captain,' he'd confided to her. 'I just want to be myself and take care of *me*.' But she didn't want him to remain a loner because that wasn't helpful in a squad situation; so, gradually, she was finding ways of drawing him into the camaraderie of the Kings. Today he was responding just as she'd hoped.

'OK, let's take a break,' she called after a

wild kick led to a frantic chase down the slope towards the river. Josh and Frazer were the boys involved and Jane was surprised by the ease with which the Scottish boy overtook the very long-legged Josh. Jane had seen him as a fairly dour defender without much pace but now it seemed she'd misjudged him. But then, at this age boys could develop physically, and sometimes emotionally, almost overnight.

Josh, skidding to a halt, suddenly stumbled and went down. He stayed down, too, clutching his ankle while Frazer, swooping on the ball, turned and began punting it back up the incline. Anxiously Jane called, 'Josh, are you OK? Want any help?'

To her relief, however, he slowly got to his feet, shaking his head. With Josh she was never sure whether to go to his aid immediately or allow him to recover in his own time. Of all the squad, he was the most injury-prone, something his mother, Karen, put down to his outgrowing his strength. Karen had several times expressed her worries about the short shorts he favoured even in the wettest weather and his willingness to hurl himself into dangerous situations in the box. Nobody could ever doubt Josh's commitment to the Kings' cause.

'Just gave my ankle a bit of a turn when I slipped,' he admitted now as he rejoined the rest of the players.

'So how did you all enjoy that?' Jane enquired as the boys awaited fresh instructions.

'Great!' – 'Crazy!' – 'Mad!' – 'Good fun' – 'Impossible!' were some of the reactions. Reuben, who'd had the most work to do, was looking as relaxed as anyone and smiling genially.

'Well, it seemed to me that you were learning how to cope with things,' she said. 'I felt you were trying to go too fast, though. Sometimes in football there *is* time to put your foot on the ball, look up and make a precision pass. Everything doesn't have to take place at the speed of an express train. So we're going to have another go, only this time I want you to *jog* instead of race round the circle. Just take things *slowly*. You'll enjoy it just as much if you can give and receive a perfect pass. Reuben, are you OK to stay as playmaker or would you like a change?'

'No, it's fine by me, Coach. I like being in the middle,' he replied, confirming her belief he'd accept responsibility if he enjoyed his role.

'You can try me there anytime you want,' volunteered Danny. 'I'm two-footed, you know, and not everyone here is.'

Jane wasn't sure whether he was deliberately getting at predominantly left-footed Reuben but she gave him the benefit of the doubt. It wasn't like the Danny she knew to make spiteful comments. 'Thanks, Danny, I'll remember that,' she smiled.

The second time they all played the passing game the ball control of most of the boys really had improved. Now they seemed able to anticipate some of the sharp angles of a bad bounce and so return passes were usually more accurate. When she saw Josh wince as the ball struck him on the shin she signalled to him to drop off the roundabout.

'Look, if you've done some damage to your ankle give it a rest now,' she told him firmly. 'I've got some ice in the freezer compartment of my medical bag so we can put that on to ease the pain and prevent swelling.'

'Er, no, I'm sure I'll be all right,' Josh tried

to reassure her. 'I mean, I like this game. Don't want to give it up.'

'Your choice,' she told him. 'But stop at once if there's more pain, Josh.'

A few minutes later she called a halt to the routine and announced they'd finish off the session with some muscle-stretching exercises as the perfect way of staying fit.

'Stretching! Isn't that the sort of thing *old* people have to do to keep, er, supple?' Davey asked. 'I see them at it when I go to the gym for weight-training.'

'Davey, stretching is for *everybody*. I know for a fact that the Arsenal coach is a great believer in these exercises. He swears they've cut down injuries to his squad. And I'm sure other Premiership coaches feel the same about them.'

'OK,' Davey replied, happy with that explanation. Nobody else questioned her programme and she was thankful that Marc (Foggy) Thrale wasn't present. He was the one who had a habit of objecting to anything that was new. Tonight, however, he'd cried off with what sounded like a good excuse: a county trial for badminton, a game that had always suited Foggy's forceful personality, in Jane's opinion.

It was rather tougher than many had expected following the energetic passing game and most were thankful when she called a halt and congratulated them for all their efforts that evening.

'You've got to be fit to win the League and that's our aim,' she added. 'A half-fit team wins nothing. So just remember that when you're groaning about all the fitness work we do. Right, one other important thing. As you know, we haven't a game on Sunday so I've decided we must make the best use of that time. I've booked the five-a-side court at the leisure centre for a 10.30 kick-off. I want everybody to turn up, just as if we were playing normally. Oh yes, make sure you bring a towel with you, even if you weren't planning to have a shower afterwards. Please don't forget it.'

Nobody wanted her to leave it at that. After the initial surprise they bombarded her with questions about whether they might be going swimming afterwards or were expected to do some 'dirty work' before getting a chance to clean up.

'No, no, you're well wide of the mark,' she laughed. 'I'm not telling you now: all will be revealed on Sunday, I promise you.'

Inevitably, Dominic was the one they turned to when his mum was out of earshot. 'Come on Dom, you must know,' they pleaded with the stockily-built central defender. 'Tell us what's going to happen.'

'No idea,' insisted Dominic, shaking back his mane of reddish hair. 'She doesn't tell me anything.' He paused and then, in a quieter tone, added, 'And I don't tell her anything about us, either.'

Foggy, who'd been phoned about the Sunday meeting by Jane, had the weirdest idea about the reason for the towels. 'She wants to examine our feet to see if we're deformed,' he told his disbelieving listeners as they assembled in the entrance lobby. 'Everybody knows feet are supposed to be smelly so she'll want us to wash 'em first, otherwise she'd collapse with the stench! If you've got deformed toes or something then you're finished. You won't be able to pass the ball. And you won't pass her test!'

27

'Rubbish!' Danny retaliated hotly. 'I know Mrs Allenby is like a nurse but that doesn't make her an expert on feet, does it? You need a medical specialist for that. Honestly, Fogs, you've become insane even faster than we all expected!'

'Dom, you'll back me up, won't you?' Foggy asked.

'If you'd been at Moore's Meadow instead of playing away you'd've heard what I said about my mum,' Dominic replied quietly. 'We don't discuss the Kings. If I want to talk about the game I do it with my dad, though to be honest he's not that interested in soccer. He likes racing and boxing. So I know nothing, Foggy, OK?'

So speculation fizzled out until Jane appeared. Then, when she told them to leave their trainers and socks off, every eye swivelled towards Foggy. Had his wild guess hit the target after all? He was about to shout aloud about his brilliance when the coach started to explain what would happen.

'You're going to play in bare feet. You'll come to no harm because this is a safe and glossy floor. No wood splinters or anything like that. We'll be using a lighter ball and the idea is to caress it, to stroke it, not thump it like a cannon-ball. With everyone barefooted anyone who is accidentally kicked shouldn't even feel it. With bare feet you quickly learn to kick the ball properly. No toe-enders because that would sting. What you're doing, boys, is going right back to basics. You did very well in the passing game. Now you can make the most of what you learned. I'm sure you'll enjoy the experience.'

Foggy, eager to cash in on the success he thought he was enjoying, couldn't resist a question. 'So will you be inspecting our feet afterwards?'

'I sincerely hope not!' she replied so strongly that everyone laughed. 'I told you, Marc, I'm not expecting any injuries. The towels are so that you can dry your feet after washing them. They're bound to pick up some dirt even on such a shiny surface.'

Happily the entire Goal Kings' squad had turned up and so the coach was able to play four teams of four-a-side with five minutes each way. By choosing to have only four in a team, she explained, each player would have more time on the ball, more opportunity to run with it and shoot. Danny and Gareth Kingstree would play as the goalkeepers throughout the mini-tournament. The two winning semi-finalists would meet in a four-minute each-way final, so there should be no shortage of motivation out there, she concluded.

'Coach, I'm not really a goalie, you know,' Gareth complained as his team-mates got ready for action. 'I know I said to Mr Todd that I'd play anywhere but I didn't mean in goal.'

She smiled warmly at the boy with the rather prominent front teeth and the floppy fringe. 'I know, Gareth, but I can't easily find a place for you among the outfield players. I've watched you during training and you handle the ball really well. If anything happened to Danny you'd be the person I'd turn to for a goalkeeper. I honestly believe you've got a lot of potential.'

'Oh,' was all he could think to reply. Ricky Todd had never been as helpful in explaining things to him and he sensed that Mrs Allenby wasn't just making excuses. Since his family had moved to Rodale Kings he'd been desperate to win a regular place in the team but even when replacements were needed for injured or absent players he'd usually still been left out. Perhaps now, though, he'd be given his chance if he could outshine Danny Loxham.

When the boys jogged out on to the pitch or sat, legs outstretched, on the low benches lining one side of the arena, there were plenty of jokes about stick-like limbs and big feet. In fact, they all did look surprisingly different to Jane herself after being so used to seeing them in thick socks and protected by shinpads. Somehow Josh looked taller than ever and already he nearly matched her height. Davey, the striker who could leap like a salmon in spite of his own lack of height, had the most powerful-looking calf muscles, the reward for all his hours of gym work and weight-training. Joe Parbold, the strong central defender who'd broken his nose in a rugby match, actually appeared almost knock-kneed but that didn't prevent him from producing some huge clearance kicks.

Inevitably, Foggy told everyone that he was

the skipper when his team took the pitch and no one argued because it simply wasn't worth arguing about. In any case, Danny was on the opposite side so there was a vacancy for captain. The boys who were spectating weren't going to be passive; choosing one side or the other to support according to their whims they cheered vociferously or sometimes jeered a missed tackle or a dreadful shot that soared above the bar.

Jane, acting as ref and timekeeper, was impressed by the players' energy and determination. All of them seemed to be playing as if their very lives depended on it. Whether their barefootedness had anything to do with that she had no way of knowing. What was obvious was that they were enjoying themselves, much as they had done in the later stages of the passing game in Moore's Meadow.

To her delight, they weren't trying to play at what newspaper writers liked to describe as 'a hundred-miles per hour'. Players were picking out team-mates for measured passes and calculated flicks; nobody was really rushing about and they were following her instructions to 'let the ball do the work'. Even the excitable Foggy was showing restraint and when he lapsed by ballooning the ball over the bar he actually swung round to shout, 'Sorry about that.' Jane knew that he was anxious about his role in the team. He was as desperate to be a striker as he was to captain the Kings but Ricky Todd had always seen him as no more than an attacking midfielder. She could admit to herself, but to no one else, that she didn't know where to play him, mainly because lately his game had fallen away. All he could be relied upon for was to promote himself. By now she'd formed her idea of how the team would play in future. Davey Stroud and Larry Hill would operate as twin strikers with Reuben Jones playing just behind them with a licence to attack when the opening was there. She could also see new roles for Lloyd and Frazer, a player who'd been almost completely ignored by her predecessor as coach.

The first semi-final, as she thought of it, was almost finished when Gareth brought off a miraculous save from the fiercest shot so far from Davey. He had to fling himself full-length to his right to fingertip the ball away. No professional goalkeeper could have done better.

'Well done, Gareth, that was terrific!' she enthused. She knew that Davey deserved praise, too, for the ferocity of his shot but he didn't need praise as much as Gareth did in his new role.

That save made all the difference because Gareth's team won 3–2 to go through to the final. He and Danny were having to play in each match to avoid the problem of employing regular outfield players as temporary goal-keepers. That, in Jane's view, would have served no purpose; boys should continue to practise the skills they already possessed.

Kieren Kelly was easily the star of the second semi-final. His defending had been improving virtually match-by-match since he'd gained a regular place in the Kings' team. But Jane hadn't realized how ambitious he was until Jakki, his mum, had confided to her that Kieren was 'hoping to catch the eye of the county selectors'. The days when he'd worried deeply about what position he should take up at set pieces seemed to be over and he appeared to know instinctively where to be to break up attacks. He'd been the butt of the jokes about physical shapes because he certainly had the thinnest legs in the squad but he'd easily laughed them off. Now he was in masterful form, even bringing off sliding tackles to dispossess ball artists like Reuben and Dominic.

It was hard for her to know how to treat Dominic at present. Although he was playing as well as ever – and he'd been selected as player-of-the-season after switching from attack to defence – he was usually quite sub-dued, even secretive, at home. In the past she and her only son, only child, had talked a lot about the game in general and the Kings in particular. Nowadays he seemed to be trying to avoid the subject with her altogether at home or even on the way to a match. She'd made it plain to him that she would never ask him personal questions about his team-mates, just as she'd told the team that Dominic would never be her 'spy'. All the same, it was a difficult position for both of them and Jane hadn't yet worked out the best way of dealing with it. Only one thing was certain: Dominic was an essential part of the Kings' defence.

He proved it with a wonderfully skilful interception of a pass intended for Larry Hill, the Kings' most recent recruit in the forwards. Then Dominic brought the ball instantly under control, shimmied past two opponents, accelerated and finally smacked an unstoppable shot past Danny. It was as good a goal as anyone could expect to see in a four-a-side match on a small pitch and Jane yelled her congratulations, 'Great goal, Dominic!' He didn't actually turn to acknowledge her praise because he was exchanging friendly jibes with Danny, usually his closest ally in the squad. That was only relative, however, because Danny tended to be pally with everyone, as befitted a skipper.

As she watched the remainder of the game she couldn't help wondering whether the team might be improved by moving Dominic back into attack, especially if he could produce such lethal finishing on a regular basis. Then second thoughts flooded in: if she did that would the rest of the players feel that she was simply favouring her son in the way that Ricky Todd had with Alex until they fell out? She sensed that the Kings might be on the verge of achieving real success and so the last thing she wanted was to upset the balance, and the confidence, of the team. In any case, she believed they already possessed plenty of attacking options if Reuben accepted his new role and she made good use of Frazer's pace.

Dominic's goal proved decisive in the second semi-final because Danny, as athletic as ever, managed to defy everyone else with a series of stops. Danny, however, still had a role to play in the final because Gareth's teams had won both matches and clearly he couldn't play for the two of them.

'Sort of makes it a bit artificial, doesn't it, when that happens?' remarked Reuben to his coach, a comment that surprised her. Reuben had been almost as quiet in recent times as Dominic but perhaps this showed that at last he felt a true part of the Kings' set-up.

'I suppose so, Reuben,' she agreed, 'but it may not be a bad thing because Gareth is getting useful experience as a goalie. I think he shows lots of promise. To tell the truth, I was thinking we needed another goalkeeper in the squad but if Gareth can keep up this form then I won't have to look further.'

Reuben smiled. He wouldn't have dreamed of saying so but he was pleased that Mrs Allenby was willing to discuss policy matters like that with him. She seemed to have lots of good ideas and he really enjoyed playing in bare feet; he felt in the closest possible touch with the ball and that mattered to him.

With only a minute or so of the final remaining, Jane was idly thinking of how good it had all been and that, thankfully, no one had suffered any painful knock or been stamped on accidentally. Then, with a howl, Josh Rowley jumped into the air after a minor collision with Frazer and promptly sat down, nursing his left foot.

'Oh you idiot, tempting fate like that!' Jane castigated herself before blowing the whistle to halt play. Of course she should have *known* who'd be the victim if there was going to be one: Josh's proneness to injury didn't change.

Helping him to the side of the pitch she handed her whistle and stopwatch to the nearest person who wasn't playing. That happened to be Marc Thrale and his face lit up with delight at being given such an important job, a job, moreover, that had lots of authority attached to it. She pointed out how much playing time remained, though she expected to resume control herself very quickly. Foggy nodded and darted forward to restart the game with the loudest blast on a whistle anyone had heard. With the strength of his voice he hardly needed a whistle anyway.

Jane knelt and took Josh's injured foot in her lap, gently testing the toes one by one to see where the damage was as Josh himself seemed unable to locate it precisely. The tears in his eyes were brushed aside in embarrassed fashion as Jane reached for the pain-killing spray.

'Josh, I don't think any real damage has been done,' she told him comfortingly. 'It's *always* painful if you stub your toe and that's what you did, I expect. So just go and sit on the bench for the rest of the match. It's nearly over, anyway. I'm sure you'll feel OK in a moment.'

He nodded, without looking convinced, but there was no time for either of them to say more because suddenly there was a hubbub on the pitch. Foggy was gesticulating wildly and claiming: 'If I say it was a foul, it *was* a foul. I'm in charge, I'm the ref, so you've got to obey me.'

'Rubbish!' Dominic was retaliating. 'You haven't a clue what's going on, Fogs. That ball didn't go above waist-level never mind above the shoulders. Right, Dan?'

Dan, fair-minded as ever, shrugged. 'Dom, I didn't see it, mate. Oats blocked my view.'

'Listen, it's a foul, so let's get on with it,' Foggy persisted.

It was the moment for Jane to resume control. Because she hadn't seen the incident, either, she decided the best thing would be to start with a bounce up, though she didn't really know whether that figured in the rules. Nobody, however, argued with the decision. She'd been surprised by how heated the row over the height of the ball had been but no doubt that proved how competitive the Kings were.

Even when play resumed Dominic continued to mutter about Marc's officiating. 'Hasn't a clue, he's just as useless at reffing as playing,' he said to Frazer, loudly enough for Jane to hear.

'Let it go, Dominic,' she told him sharply. 'Just get on with the game.'

He did but his face showed that he wasn't pleased with the reprimand and he tossed back his hair as he usually did in an argumentative mood. His mum couldn't help wondering whether he'd say anything about it when they were at home. That depended, she supposed, on how long his resentment went on smouldering.

Two minutes later the final ended with a narrow win for Danny's team and the celebrations were as enthusiastic as if they'd won a trophy and medals, which made Jane wish she'd thought of providing some mementoes. After all, it was a long time since most of them had experienced real triumph in the Kings' purple and white strip.

All she could do was praise them for their effort and their willingness to play in a way they'd never played before. Her chief worry had been that they'd regard barefoot soccer as a waste of time or something to be treated as a joke.

'So, you really enjoyed it, did you? Apart

from poor old Josh who got a stubbed toe,' she pressed them.

'Yeah, great,' several of them responded, although she couldn't help noting that Marc and Dominic gave the impression they weren't even listening. Foggy, she realized, hadn't been pleased about surrendering control of the final to her after the disputed foul.

'Every time we have training you come up with something different,' observed Danny who, by now, was probably her biggest fan among the players. 'So have you got other new plans for us, Coach?'

'As a matter of fact, I have,' she admitted in a way that caught the attention even of those who were about to switch off their interest through tiredness or the desire to get home. 'But I can't really talk about it just now, Danny, because one or two details still have to be finalized. I can tell you this, though: it's not just another new training routine. It's much, much bigger than that. And it'll happen, all being well, on our next fixture-free weekend, which is next month. Until then, it remains a secret, boys.'

'Oh, come on, Miss, we can keep a secret,'

Reuben declared, obviously very keen indeed to hear what she had in mind.

'I'm sure you can, Reuben, but I'm not going to put you to that test. Anyway, I'm glad I've whetted your appetite. Now, let's start thinking about something much nearer, the match against Friday Bridge next week. That's the one we've got to win to set our season alight. We can't afford another failure. So, on Tuesday evening, we'll plan their downfall and our victory.'

3 Bridge to Success

Jane Allenby had lost count of the number of times the telephone had rung just as she was about to leave the house. Mostly the calls were from patients or ex-patients, many of whom just wanted to chat; it seemed to her that if you'd delivered somebody's baby they couldn't resist telling you the latest news of the child's awesome achievements. Lately, though, an increasing number of calls were about football, as was this one on the Sunday morning of the Friday Bridge game.

'Karen, good to hear from you,' she greeted Josh's mother. 'Not bad news, is it? That Josh isn't fit to play today?'

'Not quite,' Mrs Rowley said in a rather strained voice. 'But I do want to be assured that he won't be taking part in anything as risky as kicking a ball with bare feet. That toe swelled up quite badly the next day and he's limped much of the week. Perhaps he could just be a substitute today, Jane. The pitch is bound to be as hard as a rock and that won't help Josh at all, especially if he takes a tumble.'

Jane sighed, reflecting that this *was* a medical call after all! Karen was often troubled about Josh's health. She worried about him playing in the rain and now, apparently, she worried about him on a dry pitch. Because Karen was such a good supporter of the Kings, even to the extent of personally laundering the team's kit, Jane was anxious not to upset her.

'Look, Karen, I'll see he's all right, I promise. I'm sure Josh will let me know if he's suffering. I'm just sorry I didn't have ice with me last Sunday when he stubbed his toe, that would definitely have kept the swelling down. He's such a brave player, you know: gives everything. Just what the Kings need.'

'You seem to be doing things very differently from Ricky,' Karen remarked, suddenly changing tack.

'True,' agreed Jane, thinking there was no point in saying more.

'But isn't there a risk that'll unsettle some of the boys? I mean, most boys – well, girls too, come to that – prefer a set routine in their lives. If you go too far in a different direction they can lose confidence, that sort of thing.'

'Karen, I'm sure you've got a point but I haven't time to debate it with you now,' Jane said firmly. 'I'm sorry but I've got to get to the ground and prepare for the match. Don't worry, I'll keep a careful check on Josh's health. I don't want to lose one of my best players through injury. Bye, Karen.'

Dominic, who'd been hovering by the kitchen door throughout the conversation, frowned as she put down the phone. 'Josh isn't one of our *best* players. He makes loads of mistakes. Kieren and I usually have to cover up for him. He just gets away with things because he never stops charging about all over the pitch, looking as if he's involved in everything.'

That view really surprised her. 'Dominic, it's not like you to criticize your team-mates. Have you and Josh fallen out or something?'

'Course not! He's not a mate of mine at any time. I'm just telling you what some of the other guys think. They think like I do. You seem to think Josh is such a star player you have to keep chatting to him and, er, well, *pandering* to his imaginary injuries. Mum, Josh is *not* a star player.'

'Right, I'll remember that, Dom,' she replied briskly. She wouldn't dream of raising the matter now but she couldn't help wondering whether Dominic was exhibiting signs of jealousy. Or did he simply resent attention she gave to any of the other players? Was his comment about Josh just a sign he felt she was neglecting him, her own son? It was something she'd have to think about. 'Come on, we've got to be off. I've got a few things to say to everyone before kick-off.'

Several of the players' parents and other supporters were already present when she arrived at the Kings' home ground and she deliberately made a point of having a chat with some of them. She wanted to delay her entrance into the dressing-room to give players time to get changed and to avoid embarrassing them. It seemed she needn't have bothered because although some of them were still half-dressed when she walked in they didn't exhibit any signs of dismay. By now, of course, they were used to her ministrations when they'd been injured so she hoped that henceforth they'd always feel at ease in her presence however they were dressed. A coach could hardly be expected to stay out of the dressing-room until the last seconds before the team went on to the pitch.

'So, Kings, this is the start of our new future together,' she told them with the brightest of smiles. 'And it's going to be wonderful because we're going to win today and we're going to go on, winning and winning and winning.'

She stopped at that point to see how they'd react. For a few moments nobody said a word because they were all so surprised by that promise. Neither of their previous two coaches, Sam Saxton and Ricky Todd, had been so glowingly optimistic. Both, in fact, had often displayed caution and even a touch of pessimism.

Danny, however, literally rose to the occasion. Springing to his feet he yelled, 'That's right. Kings rule! Kings rule for ever!' And most of the others joined in to sing out the Kings' by now traditional battle-cry. Jane couldn't help noticing that Dominic wasn't among them but then he wasn't the demonstrative type. Neither was Reuben but he was on his feet even though he hadn't yet put on shorts or socks. Foggy managed to join in but with less enthusiasm than usual. Jane guessed that was because she'd already informed him he'd only be on the subs' bench today. After being given the ref's whistle during the barefoot game he'd assumed he'd be an automatic choice in teams she picked, and now he knew he wasn't.

'Well, you're in good voice so let's hope your play matches it,' she told them before simply adding, 'We only just scraped through against Friday Bridge last time, so this time I'd rather not be a nervous wreck up to the last minute!'

That previous occasion was the Final of the Highlea Sunday League Knock-out Cup and the Kings had won on a penalty shoot-out in the most dramatic fashion. Earlier in the game Danny had scored his spectacular goal as he was forever recalling when the game was mentioned.

'Might get another today, I feel in the mood,' Danny boasted to Dominic as they trotted out on to the bone-dry pitch. 'I reckon the Bridge are a lucky team for me.'

'Better be careful,' counselled his fellow-defender. 'Mum – I mean, the coach – well, she said not to give anything away at the back. We've got to see how it works with Oats given freedom to charge forward down the left.'

Danny's grey eyes narrowed and he flicked his chewing-gum from one side of his mouth to the other. 'She didn't tell *you* to tell *me* not to go outside my penalty area, did she?' he wanted to know.

'Course not! She only tells me what she tells everybody, Danny. I wish you'd all get it into your heads that I don't get any special treatment just because I live in the same house as the coach! I knew you'd all think that, which is why you guys shut up like clams when I come into the dressing-room. I'm telling you again, I wouldn't pass on a word of what you guys talk about. Honest!'

'OK, Dom, I get the message,' responded Danny, reaching across to slap his team-mate on the back with the gloves he was carrying but probably wouldn't wear today. 'I promise we won't ever exclude you again, if that's what we've been doing.'

'Great!' exclaimed Dominic, smiling for the first time since he'd arrived at the ground.

The omens for success were good. The Kings won the toss and therefore automatically decided to play towards the cricket pavilion end, the direction they always favoured in the first half; and the Friday Bridge left-winger who'd caused their defence so many problems with the quality of his crosses and his speed in the Cup Final wasn't playing. 'The Bridge', as they were popularly known, came from a small riverside village not far from Rodale Kings. It got its name from its original inhabitants who all gave up their Fridays to help construct a bridge to span the river.

Their team, colourfully attired in harlequin-style shirts with red and yellow squares and scarlet shorts, were the first to attack when the young female referee set the game in motion. In perfectly ordered style, the Kings' midfielders and back-four retreated to mark opponents as the visitors swarmed forward. Jane found herself hurrying along the touch-line to keep up with play, something she'd hardly ever done when Ricky was in charge. Now, though, she felt completely involved in everything that was happening in front of her. She'd told herself not to shout much whatever the state of the game because she believed that the boys weren't usually helped by receiving instructions in the midst of hectic play. Congratulations and general encouragement were a different matter.

Fortunately, the Friday Bridge striker overran the ball after being nudged off-balance by a tackle from Kieren and Danny was off his line like lightning to scoop it up and then, overarm, throw it to Frazer. The throw was so well-aimed that Frazer merely had to run on to it before starting his own attack down the left flank.

'Keep going, Frazer!' Jane yelled and he was near enough to her to do exactly as he was told. When challenged he had the presence of mind to slow, screen the ball from his opponent and then accelerate again.

Already Davey Stroud and Larry Hill were running on parallel courses through the middle and with the Bridge defence at full-stretch they were praying for a cross. Oats hardly looked up before sweeping the ball towards them from a point well inside the Bridge half; Davey, poorly marked, had no difficulty in suddenly darting sideways to pick up possession. In spite of his small size Davey could produce a devastating change of pace. He produced it now to cut inside the box before flicking the ball to Larry on his right. And Larry tried a trick he'd actually learned from Davey in training: the moment the ball was at his feet he tried a shot at goal before the goalkeeper might expect it.

The shot was on target. Unhappily for Larry, however, it was just too near to the goalie who managed to parry it but was then unable to prevent it bouncing over the byline for a corner.

'Well done, Kings! Keep pressing!' Jane sang out among the applauding supporters.

Josh was up for the corner but on this occasion the ball eluded him and Friday Bridge's equally tall central defender was able to hoof it out of the box. Cunningly, Reuben had held back and he seized control when the ball came down invitingly a metre in front of him. Promptly Reuben curled the ball back into the penalty area where Josh was able to rise and with a perfect looping header send it over the goalkeeper and into the back of the net.

Like the rest of the Kings, Jane flung her arms into the air to celebrate a goal within three minutes of the kick-off. Then the ecstasy died almost as quickly as the fans realized that the referee's scissors-like waving indicated that the goal was disallowed. Her assistant's flag had gone up for off-side and that was that. Josh's shoulders slumped and it was a moment or two before he remembered he was needed for defensive duties.

'Hard luck, Josh. Good header all the same,' Jane called to him. She'd already looked round the ground to see whether Karen Rowley was present but there was no sign of her.

'Perfect start for you, Jane, if that goal had counted,' murmured Serena Colmer who had come to stand beside her. 'But the boys look sharp today, don't they? Must be due to your very inventive training methods!'

'Thanks, Serena, that's kind of you,' replied Jane, glancing at Lloyd's mum who, for once, had abandoned her favourite multi-coloured skirts in favour of very trim red shorts, perhaps in response to the brilliant weather.

That first goal was not long delayed, however. Already Friday Bridge's defence was exhibiting signs of worry for it was no longer as watertight as it had been in the Cup Final. On another raid down the left flank, Oats' pace simply unhinged the two defenders who'd been told to cover that zone. This time Oats, after turning them, hit a long pass into the middle where Lloyd patiently allowed the ball to bounce before hooking it towards the edge of the box where Davey was darting in behind a central defender. Sensing real danger the goalkeeper rushed from his line. Davey, who'd taken a quick look round, called 'Reuben!' and slid the ball at a sharp angle back to his fair-haired team-mate.

Now with a vast amount of goalmouth to aim at, Reuben wasn't going to miss an opening like that. His precise left-foot drive took the ball high into the unguarded net.

'Oh, what a well-worked goal!' enthused Serena, well aware that Lloyd had been an important link in the chain of attack. 'Reuben looks as if he could fly over the moon, doesn't he?'

He did. Because he hadn't been a regular scorer with any team he'd ever played for, his first goal for the Kings was something he really had dreamed about but that had been only a toe-poke in a crowded penalty area. The reality was so much better as team-mates swooped to shower him with congratulations. As the ref rounded them up, urging them to get on with the game, Reuben couldn't resist looking across at Jane and raising his thumbs. After all, she was the one who'd shown faith in him and given him a new role as part of the cutting edge.

Jane, too, was glowing. Her own belief in the pace and directness of Frazer's running and the attacking skills of Reuben couldn't have been realized in better or swifter fashion. It was almost uncanny how the goal had been scored, almost as if the boys had committed to memory their orders for a military-style operation and carried them out to perfection. Apart from sharing in Reuben's personal delight she was thrilled with Davey's un-selfish contribution. It would have been quite natural for him to try to score himself from that position. Instead, he'd heeded her instructions to 'talk to each other' and set up a chance for a team-mate who was slightly better placed. At that moment she felt she really was a genuine football coach. Then, wryly, she grinned for she supposed that the trick now was to keep this success going.

In one sense, she had no worries because the second goal arrived within five minutes so that the dream start against the Bridge became brighter still. This time the assault on the visitors' goal was down the right flank with Kieren Kelly doing his best to emulate Oats' style. Exchanging passes with Reuben and then Larry, he couldn't resist the temptation to go another metre: and that was where his run ended as a Bridge defender took the ball off Kieren before deciding to turn it back to his goalkeeper, better positioned to make a good clearance. Not expecting a back-pass at that stage the goalie reacted hastily, swung at the ball with his right foot and succeeded only in sending it spinning wildly across the penalty area.

Davey Stroud's electric acceleration might have been designed for such a situation. Moving sooner and faster than anyone else, he reached the ball ahead of everyone and needed only the simplest of touches to steer it into the gaping net. He even had time to see the expression of sheer horror on the goal-keeper's face as the boy in a yellow sweater registered the outcome of his error.

'The way things are going it must be my lad's turn to score next. This lot are just ripe for carving up, aren't they?' remarked the man who'd come to stand next to Jane. He was Taylor Hill, owner of a very popular bistro in the High Street and father of Larry, Davey's co-striker, a fairly recent addition to the team.

'Well, they're certainly not the team we beat in the Cup Final,' Jane agreed. 'But I'm sure they won't give us another goal as soft as that one. They're bound to get their act together soon.'

'Doesn't matter how much they improve, my lad'll sort them out,' declared Mr Hill, never slow to promote Larry's interests. 'He'll get a goal soon, you'll see.'

He did, too. Supplied with another precise pass, this time from Dominic, Larry powered through the centre, looking for all the world like an exhibition of elbows and knees in motion. Yet, in spite of his ungainliness as a runner, he was hard to dispossess and two attempts by determined defenders were hopeless. Then, when another challenge loomed up, Larry exchanged a one-two with Davey, called for the return to make sure he got it, and then blasted the ball at the goalkeeper. The match was becoming a nightmare for the goalie because this time he failed to do more than allow the ball to bounce off his chest. So Larry, following up, was able to collect the ball again, waltz round the stricken opponent, and bury the ball in the back of the net.

'Told you!' crowed Taylor Hill.

'You did – well done,' laughed an equally pleased coach. 'That was a wonderful example of his determination, he really deserved a goal.'

Inevitably, Friday Bridge's coach was looking angry at what he knew were inexcusable lapses of concentration or sheer incompetence. Although she'd never experienced such poor play from her team, Jane could sympathize with his attitude. After all, she'd seen how Ricky Todd had been affected by the Kings' disappointing performances at the start of the season. Thoughts of her predecessor caused her to scan the opposite touch-line in case he'd turned up as a spectator. There was no sign of him and she was rather glad about that; they'd have been bound to talk at some point and it would have been difficult not to gloat over the changes she knew she'd brought about in the Kings' play.

Just before half-time the home side scored yet again and this time it was Lloyd who put the ball in the net. Once again Reuben had a foot in it. When he took a free kick following a clumsy tackle on Larry he drove the ball well wide of the penalty area for Kieren to pump it into the middle or even try a long-range shot. The ploy took the Bridge defence by surprise because they'd been expecting a floater over the top of their wall. Unmarked, Kieren went for glory with a shot as hard as any he'd hit. It flew over everyone until, at the last moment, it dipped a fraction, struck the crossbar and bounced down. The goalkeeper flailed at it to try to clear his lines somehow but it really was his unlucky day. For he could only knock it sideways to Lloyd who very coolly steered it into the net by the base of the near post. While his fellow defenders berated the haunted goalie for his failings, Lloyd practically turned cartwheels on his way back to the centre.

In the coach's eyes Lloyd had always shown plenty of promise but somehow he didn't play consistently well. When things had gone badly for the Kings he'd been the most depressed member of the team. Perhaps if the Kings enjoyed a real run of success the speedy midfielder would really blossom.

'So, what d'you think of our performance so far?' she asked, turning to the boys on the bench behind her.

'Great!' said Gareth Kingstree, eyes shining with genuine pleasure. 'We're murdering 'em. Could get a record score today, Coach.'

There couldn't have been a greater contrast in Marc Thrale's response. 'They're just giving us goals 'cos their goalie's complete rubbish,' he frowned. 'Friday Bridge are so bad we ought to have got double the number of goals.'

Jane waited a moment because she was sure he was going to add something to the effect that if he'd been on the pitch he'd've scored four all by himself. He didn't, perhaps having sensed that he'd already said quite enough. 'I don't think you're being very kind to your team-mates, Marc,' she told him. 'You've looked pretty miserable ever since the match started. Not sulking, are you?'

'Course not!' he replied sharply. 'I don't sulk, just want to get on the pitch, that's all. You going to put me on soon, Mrs Allenby?'

'Haven't decided yet,' she said, not quite truthfully. 'Have to see how well we do in the second half. The main thing is to avoid injuries on a firm pitch like this. The point to remember, Marc, is that you're in the squad. The Kings aren't just the eleven players on the pitch at any one time.'

That half-hearted vote of confidence didn't really satisfy him but he wasn't going to say anything more for the present; privately he was beginning to wonder whether he should have listened to Alex Todd a couple of weeks earlier, when he'd asked him if he was interested in joining another team or even helping to start a new one.

Half-time arrived without any additions to the score sheet. Friday Bridge's defence had tightened up, although the goalkeeper was as nervous as a new boy at school when anyone approached him. He feared he was going to be replaced by one of the substitutes in the second half and he was right.

'You're playing brilliantly but don't ease up whatever you do,' Jane told her team as they sipped energy drinks or ate bananas provided as their interval refreshments by the Kings' Friends' committee. 'At the end of the season goal difference might make all the difference to us and our position in the League.'

'So d'you want me to move up into attack more often, Coach?' enquired Josh.

She shook her head very firmly. 'Definitely not! Preventing goals is just as important as ever when we are on top. If we let them back into the game and they score a couple of goals, well, anything could happen. We've got a good pattern of play, so let's stick by it, boys.'

By the start of the second half the crowd numbers appeared to have increased, almost as if word had got round the village that the Kings were enjoying a goal spree and ought to be watched. Jane, still keeping an eye open for a sighting of either of her predecessors, was pleased to see that Sallie McKinnon, Frazer's mother, had now turned up, accompanied by a tall slim girl with her hair in a blonde ponytail.

'This is Andrea, Frazer's sister,' said Sallie as they joined Jane on the touchline. 'Couldn't get away earlier because I was fixing some party food. But I know the team's winning. So how's Frazer playing?'

'Oh, really well, Sallie. He's set up one of the goals. Honestly, I'd no idea until recently how fast he can run – and run with the ball, I mean. Now I'm trying to make the most of that by getting him to adopt an attacking role down the wing. It's worked so far.'

'I'm sure Andrea could have told you about Frazer's talents. They're always out training together, those two.'

Jane turned to her. 'Oh, you like football, then, Andrea?'

'Love it. It's just great.'

'So would you like to play for a team? Or maybe you already do?'

'Definitely,' replied Andrea so forcefully her ponytail bobbed up and down. 'But girls don't seem to get into boys' teams around here, just like it was when we were back home in Scotland.'

Jane, still keeping an eye on play but keenly interested in this conversation with the willowy, green-eyed girl, remarked, 'But what about a girls' team? Maybe –'

'Not interested in that,' Andrea cut in. 'The girls I know round here are too soft to play *real* football. So I just play mixed football when I get the chance.'

'Oh,' said Jane, slotting that information into a mental cubby-hole until there was time to review it properly.

'Knows her own mind, this one,' smiled Sallie. 'I'm sure she'll get what she wants one of these days.'

By now Jane was concentrating fully on the game because Kieren, doing his best to match Frazer's skills as a raider, had made such good progress down the right flank that both Kings' strikers were calling for a cross. Kieren, however, had picked out Reuben, loitering on the far side of the box, and the ball was whipped across to the unmarked midfielder.

Reuben was already gliding towards the ball and, skilfully taking it under control with one flick of his left foot, twisted past a static opponent. Davey, sensing an opening, called for, and received, the sort of pass he dreamed about: on the ground and a metre ahead of him. The dismayed Bridge defence was in disarray as Davey accelerated through the middle. The goalkeeper feared the worst and edged forward, guessing he'd be into a one-on-one with the short, stocky opponent any second now. Reuben hadn't stopped running and when he called for a return pass, he got it, to his surprise. But he wasn't too surprised to take the ball in his stride, switch it from one foot to the other, and then lift it over the goalkeeper's head. Even before it entered the net Reuben was whirling away, arm raised in triumph, before joining Davey for a celebratory hug.

The Friday Bridge coach covered his face with his hands. Plainly, nothing he'd said to his team at half-time had been of the slightest use. The marking was atrocious, the tackling non-existent. How on earth would he be able to pick them up again after a defeat on this scale? For he feared there were more goals yet to come for the rampant Kings. In fact, there was only one more but that was bad enough because it was an own goal put into the back of the net by the substitute goalkeeper. Still, it was hardly his fault because a full-back, desperate to clear the danger in a scramble almost on the goal-line, kicked wildly and saw the ball ricochet from his keeper's left shoulder and loop over the line.

'Can hardly believe everything's gone so well as this,' murmured Jane as the final whistle shrilled. 'I mean, 6–0! Can't remember the last time we won so easily. Yet Friday Bridge are a decent side, though they certainly played poorly today.'

'Jane, I'm sure the boys will say you've shown them what they're capable of,' said Serena, giving the new coach a congratulatory kiss. 'Everybody could see how they were *enjoying* themselves. That's the big difference from, well, from the days they were playing when Ricky was in charge. Well done!'

'I think we had luck on our side, though,' Jane suggested. 'Their goalie couldn't do a thing right and the sub didn't have a ghost of a chance with the last goal. Lucky for us.'

'Maybe, Jane, but they all count, don't they? That's what Lloyd says and he's right. Folk just remember that a goal was scored and who scored it. Nobody involved really bothers with the luck side of it.'

'I suppose so,' Jane agreed, turning to accept congratulations from other parents and supporters. Everyone was thrilled by the scale of the victory over a team that currently was higher in the League than the Kings.

'Just what we needed to give our season a kick-start,' said Clark Kelly, Kieren's dad. Grinning, he added: 'It'll put our boys on a real high for the Highlands! Can't wait for that.'

'Hey, you haven't told Kieren about that, have you? It's supposed to be a surprise when I announce it in a few minutes. And we're not going as far north as that, you know!'

The boys were still bubbling with their success when she reached the dressing-room. Reuben was a revelation because in the past everyone had been aware of his liking for solitude and his general unwillingness to say much about anything to anyone. Now he was leading the singing in a chorus of 'We're going to win the League, We're going to win the League!' However, like the rest of the squad he fell silent when Jane clapped her hands to gain attention. They never could quite guess what she might tell them. In any case, they'd experienced the shock of being criticized by their previous coach after a victory! So anything was possible when it came from someone who'd arranged for a training session on a meadow as smooth as a ploughed field and then had them playing in bare feet.

'That was the best I've seen you play – well, since I took over!' she joked and one or two managed to laugh. 'So, you're going to get a special reward. We're going off on a weekend trip to Scotland to play a team called Aberlyn Thistle. We'll be staying in the homes of the Thistle players and so we'll be sharing lots of time with them. Your families all know about this and if none of you've heard a whisper about it then they've kept the secret perfectly. Well, what d'you think of that?'

'Fantastic!' – 'Terrific!' – 'Can't wait!' were predictable responses. Frazer's was the most original, 'Hey, I'm away home! Thought I'd left Scotland for ever. Well, sort of. But where's Aberlyn, Coach? It's not in the Highlands where I come from.'

'It's a long way south of the Highlands,

Frazer. Just over the border from England, in fact. It's on the coast and there's a sandy beach so there's lots to enjoy besides the football. The Kings' Friends' committee have organized most of it and your families will get final details during the week. Oh yes, we'll be travelling by coach but there'll be board games to play and books to read so you won't be bored. Well, you'd better not be! A bored footballer is a bad footballer. Remember that! OK now – any urgent questions before I leave you?'

Reuben's smile had faded as he enquired, 'Coach, will I have a room to myself in this house where I'll be staying? Won't have to share, will I?'

She could guess why he was asking that. The eldest of a large family which included a recently born baby, Reuben was often required to shoulder lots of responsibilities at home where, it was now clear, he didn't have a bedroom to himself.

'I can't give you a definite answer now, Reuben, but I'll look into it, do my best to see that you have some privacy,' she promised.

Just as she was on the point of leaving she

noticed her son's puzzled expression and decided it was a good time to establish an important point. 'One last thing,' she called, 'in case you're wondering, this is just as much a surprise to Dominic as to the rest of you. Remember what I told you when I took over; every single one of you is treated in exactly the same way – by me, at least. Right, enjoy your discussions.'

As she made her way to her car, Jane reflected on both the match and the boys' reactions to the news of the weekend away. There was no doubt that Friday Bridge weren't the force they'd been in the Cup Final so perhaps this easy victory wasn't really a guide to the Kings' future. Maybe they'd fail to beat even slightly stronger opposition. Only time would tell.

Meanwhile, the Scottish experience might offer a few pointers.

4 Partnerships and Problems

'Come on, Andi, you can finish that magazine later,' Frazer called to his sister from their back garden. 'I really need some more practice before I go to Scotland. Need to get in some good crosses. You never know, I just might catch the eye of some selector who turns up for the Thistle game.'

Andrea came out to join him only moments later. Already dressed in football shirt and shorts like him she rarely needed to be cajoled into a kick-about even though at present she was depressed at not being allowed to accompany him on the Kings' weekend trip.

'You know, Mum could've let me off that violin lesson on Saturday morning,' she grumbled as they made their way to the bottom of the garden where they'd set out what they both called their 'training pitch'. 'I mean, she *knows* footie means as much to me as it does to you. *And* she helped set up the trip in the first place because she knows so many people there. It's just not fair.'

'Life's like that,' Frazer replied laconically. 'Your turn'll come, Andi. Bound to. Anyway, I don't expect she'll let me go with *you* if you get picked for that netball tournament in Manchester. Oh come on, stand a bit further back than that. I'm aiming for the back post.'

She realized she wasn't really in the mood for this but now she was out here she might as well make the most of it. But she hadn't retreated quite far enough, for one left-foot drive struck her so hard in the chest it almost knocked her off balance.

'Hey, you're supposed to hit it *over* me!' she protested. 'I don't want a flat chest, you know.'

'Well, you've got one, haven't you?' he said unsympathetically.

'No, I haven't – look,' she replied, smoothing her shirt over her chest to provide the evidence. 'You don't notice *anything*, do you, unless it's about football?'

'Yes I do! I notice other girls,' he claimed.

'Oh yeah, I'll bet you do, brother. Which ones?'

'Er, Sophie, Danny's girl-friend – I think. Got masses of luscious brown hair. Not a bit like yours.'

Her eyes narrowed. 'Danny? Your goalie, you mean? Has he really got a girl-friend?'

'Well, we all know he fancies her but I've not seen them together. Why, are *you* interested in him?'

'What a *stupid* question,' Andrea retorted although she didn't raise her voice. 'Come on I thought you wanted to practise crosses. So get them on the right target in future.'

Foggy was furious. He couldn't believe how bad his luck was, as he kept telling everyone. Just when he'd got over his injuries and poor form and a new coach who didn't understand him, *this* had to happen.

'But why does Aunt Julia have to get married on that day? Why can't she wait another week or something?' he stormed at his mother.

'Because it's the most convenient day for her and James,' Mrs Thrale replied placidly. 'Marc, it's no good going on about this. Everything's finalized. So you can't go to Scotland. I'm sorry but there it is.'

Foggy never gave up easily. 'But the wedding's nothing to do with *me*. I won't be wanted for anything, will I?'

'You might be an usher or something like that. But that's not the point. Weddings are all about families and families have to be united at weddings. So that's that.'

'United is the name of a football team and I should be playing for a football team, not messing about at a wedding,' Foggy grumbled, but knew he'd lost this match.

Lloyd was worried about food. Tuna was what he liked above all other foods and if that wasn't available then he'd prefer another kind of fish and one with oil in it would be best of all. But would the people he was staying with in Scotland be able to provide those dishes? Would they insist he ate red meat or chicken or stuff like that, if that was what everyone else was eating? Worst of all, would they give him something called haggis, a speciality of Scotland? Larry Hill's dad, who ran the bistro in the High Street, had told Larry that haggis was made of the heart and lungs and liver of a sheep, all minced up and boiled with oatmeal and suet and that it resembled a large, dumpy sausage.

'Ugh, I can't eat that, Mum,' he declared when they were discussing the weekend away.

'Well, you won't have to, Lloydie,' she re-assured him. 'You'll have to explain that you're best off not eating spicy things and have to stick to fish and simple dishes. Your Grandad told you to do that because he had a heart problem and it might run in the family. No one can argue with that, Lloydie!'

'Hey, I'll do it!' he said, cheering up immediately. 'That's great, Mum. Thanks!'

'You're welcome,' Serena Colmer smiled. She had her fingers crossed she hadn't tempted fate in telling him that. Most of it was true, after all.

Davey Stroud was wondering whether he'd be lucky enough to share accommodation with Reuben. Although he'd heard Reuben's request to Mrs Allenby to have a room to himself wherever he was staying there might be a possibility of being in the same house. Then Davey would have the perfect opportunity to discuss with his fair-haired team-mate how they could work together to build up a brilliant partnership on the pitch.

None of the Kings' players was quite so ambitious as Davey, not even Alex Todd when he had the chief striker's role during his dad's spell as coach. Davey was convinced that he had a real future as an international in spite of his lack of height. He had pace and ball control and could jump higher than anyone in the team. What's more, Kevin Keegan, the former England star and top manager, had said no player should ever be overlooked just because of his physical size.

In training and, especially, on the evidence of the match against Friday Bridge it was plain to him that he and Reuben were in tune with one another. Reuben could deliver exactly the kind of ammunition Davey needed to shoot a hatful of goals. If they could just have a little time together on their own then Davey was sure he could convince his quietly-spoken team-mate to play things his way.

What Davey didn't know was that, coincidentally, his fellow striker, Larry Hill, was thinking much the same thing about his own future prospects.

* * *

'Dad, can I ask you a favour?' said Danny as David Loxham switched off one of his favourite TV news programmes and looked meaningfully at his watch. 'Could I take your mobile phone with me to Scotland? I *swear* I won't use it unless I have to – except to call you, of course.'

His father frowned. 'They're expensive things, you know. Costs a fortune for even a short call, especially over that distance. And if you lost it and someone else started using it I could be in debt for hundreds of pounds before I could put a stop on it. No –'

'But Dad, I *don't* lose things, do I? I'm always careful, you know that. Oh go on, *please*. Listen, I'll switch it on at just the times we've agreed so that *you* can ring me and find out how I'm doing. I mean, I am in a sort of foreign country and you'll be all on your own at home, won't you? Unless Mum suddenly comes back.'

Danny knew very well that any reference to his mother, who'd been missing for two years, was nearly always guaranteed to gain his dad's sympathetic support. He didn't like to play on it but was desperate to get the phone so that he could be sure of ringing Sophie at the right times and in complete privacy.

'I'll think about it, Danny,' was, however, as much as his dad would promise for the present.

Dominic was wandering aimlessly around the house when his mother came home after visiting her final patient for the day. He couldn't settle to anything and his thoughts kept returning to the trip to Scotland. He wasn't sure he was going to be able to cope with seeing his mother take charge of everybody, and organize everything, for an entire weekend.

'Dad not home yet?' she greeted him cheerfully, though she was feeling tired after a long day.

Dominic shook his head. 'Seems to be getting later and later these days. Bit like you, Mum. He says he's getting lots more houses to deliver to because people are lazy, don't want to do their own shopping. Good job *he* doesn't play sport: he'd be too tired for that after finishing work.'

'Suppose *I'd* better think about getting tonight's meal then. That'll make a change for you. Anything you fancy?'

He shrugged. 'Not really. I'll go for whatever you've got.'

Jane gave her only child a calculating look. 'Darling, is everything all right? You seem a bit down in the dumps. To tell the truth, you've been that way for a little time. Is it still all about my taking over as coach? That you feel excluded or something like that?'

'No, no, not really,' he said quickly, not feeling able to admit to the truth of that idea. 'I'm just wondering what it's going to be like in Scotland, what's going to happen, who we'll meet. That sort of stuff. I expect the other guys know more about it than I do.'

'No they *don't*,' she responded emphatically. 'I tell them no more than I tell you. I promised that when I took over the job and I haven't wavered. You and your dad know I'm a great believer in fair play, fair shares, fair everything. That's always been my way in the family, too. You must know that.'

'OK, I suppose so,' Dominic said resignedly.

After a brief pause Mrs Allenby added, 'But

maybe I could stretch things a little and just hint at something I think you'll enjoy. Nobody else has been told about it yet but if all goes well and to plan then you'll be having a game of beach soccer in addition to the main game on Sunday morning.'

'*Beach* soccer? The sort of thing they do in Brazil? All those TV programmes about Brazil always show loads of players taking part in a game on the sands right next to the ocean.'

'Almost certainly like that,' she agreed. 'And you should enjoy that because you always liked the sands when you were little. Couldn't get you to stop building castles or bringing bucketfuls of the stuff home with you. So is that something to look forward to, football on the beach?'

'Oh yes,' he said, brightening immediately. 'Can't wait!'

5 Soccer on the Sands

The sea was astonishingly calm in the bay and Dominic wished it wasn't. It had been just as calm when several of them had been out in a boat owned by one of the host families and they had all felt it was about as exciting as sailing on a pond. Even now, in the middle of the afternoon of this Indian summer day, the sun was reflecting off the gentle waves that lapped sands that were almost white.

'I thought they had fierce storms with lashing gales and mile-high waves,' remarked Reuben who claimed that meteorology was one of his favourite subjects. He might like to be a weather-forecaster on TV because he wouldn't have to work more than about five minutes a day *in total*. 'Isn't that why they have lighthouses like that one out there to warn ships about rocks they could smash into?'

'Probably,' Davey agreed. 'But the forecast

said this spell of good weather is going to last into next week, so we're not going to see anything dramatic, Reuben.'

'Oh well, we'll just have to make the football exciting, won't we?' said Frazer with a grin. 'You boys have got to enjoy your visit to the greatest country in the world. We want our visitors to return home feeling they've had a terrific time.'

'It'll only be exciting if we win,' Danny pointed out. 'I mean, we haven't come two hundred miles to lose, have we? So what's the opposition like? You should know, Oats, it's your patch.'

Frazer, however, shook his head. 'No idea. Paul, the boy I'm staying with, says they don't play much on the sands and they don't play much five-a-side either. He seems more into fishing than football, actually.'

'They're just kidding you, Oats,' Kieren claimed. 'They've probably got a secret team of three-metre-tall guys with giant-sized boots to kick our heads off! They've been waiting for us because nobody else in Scotland'll play 'em. All the rest of the Scots are scared to death of Aberlyn Thistle!'

'No way! In any case, they can't wear boots because this game is on sand and is played in bare feet,' Dominic revealed. 'So we'll be on level terms there.'

'I didn't know that,' said Danny, eyes narrowing. 'How d'you know that, Dom? Did your mum tell you?'

'Er no, I picked it up from Mr McCune,' was the hasty answer. 'He's their coach and that's where I'm staying. Mum's staying with someone else because she thought that'd be fairer. Listen, guys, he – Mr McCune – says this sand soccer is just a fun thing, it's not supposed to be a rehearsal for the real thing, the match against Thistle tomorrow morning.'

'Huh, he may think that but I'm here to win, just like Danny said,' Davey declared. 'And Reuben and I are going to get hat-tricks, right Reuben?'

'If you say so,' grinned Reuben, unaware that he was getting worried looks from Larry. 'I really like this barefoot stuff. You can control the ball much better than in boots.'

'Glad to hear you say that, Reuben, justifies all my training sessions so far,' said a delighted voice just behind them. They all

84

swung round, startled, though they knew at once who'd spoken.

'Oh, hi, Coach,' Reuben responded. 'Didn't hear you creeping up on us like that.'

'Well, that's the beauty of soft sand, you can manage all sorts of things on sand you couldn't manage elsewhere,' replied Jane, looking as happy as she sounded. In the true manner of soccer coaches she was carrying a football and now she neatly drop-kicked it to land a good distance ahead of them. But she wasn't bare-footed, she was in white trainers.

'D'you know, I felt we were missing something but couldn't think what it was,' joked Danny who, half an hour earlier, had succeeded in making his first phone call from Scotland to Sophie and was again in an euphoric state. 'Now I've remembered and there it is, a ball! Nice kick, Coach. If you ever fancy playing in goal, let me know. OK with you, Dom?'

'Definitely not! If Mum's in goal we could let in any number of soft goals,' said her only son.

Jane shot him a grateful glance for the ease with which he'd made that response and then announced, 'Well, I can tell that the sea air of Bonnie Scotland is doing you all a power of good, judging by your mood. That was the idea. If you're enjoying yourself, if you're happy with the way things are going, then you'll play well, too. I know that probably sounds like a speech from a coaching manual but it's true. Dominic quoted Mr McCune quite correctly because Mr McCune told me the same thing when we set up this visit: beach soccer is for fun. But it's still got rules because every proper game's got to have them.'

'Oh, Miss, you're not going to tell us them all, are you?' complained Larry, anxious to establish himself as an important figure in the team. Since getting into the side on a regular basis he feared that if he didn't speak up for himself he'd be overshadowed by more extrovert players like Danny, Foggy, Davey and Lloyd. He was thankful Foggy was missing from this trip. 'I just want to get on with the game. I'm desperate for the green light like those Formula One drivers!'

Most of them laughed at that as Jane complimented him, 'Nice imagery, that, Larry. And you're right, there's no need to list everything, especially as most things are similar to League rules. Just two you must remember, though. One, there's no offside. Two, you're allowed to kick only the ball. You don't kick an opponent and you don't kick sand *at* him. If you get sand in your eyes it can be nasty. So, anybody who deliberately kicks sand up is sent off, no argument allowed. OK?'

'OK, Coach,' Oats started to say when Jane held up a hand.

'No more talk, Frazer. The opposition's arrived. Right on cue – or do I mean McCune!'

Dominic was the one who raised his eyes heavenwards at that semi-pun. He'd already decided it was about time he started to impress the coach, too, so if there was no offside then he thought he'd help himself to a few goals. After all, when he'd first played for the Kings it had been as a striker until his first coach had converted him to defending.

As it turned out there wasn't really time for any player to make plans because the entire game was played at a furious pace, rather like a playground kickabout with everybody wanting the ball in order to do something the rest would remember and talk about for ages.

The playing area was just as congested and even the goal-posts were makeshift, just thin sticks brought along by the coach and driven into the sand to remain as vertical as possible. A crossbar, of course, was simply an imaginary line at an appropriate height. Inevitably rows broke out about whether the ball would have passed beneath it and only the ref could resolve them.

It didn't take the Kings long to identify their toughest opponent. Gordon already had the thighs of a rugby prop and the ferocious tackling to match. At one point he even knocked a team-mate over in his eagerness to bring down Reuben who was cleverly about to set up a chance for Davey. On that occasion Davey received the pass and duly dispatched the ball between the posts to put the Kings two-up. Next time, however, Davey himself was the victim, flattened as flat as could be when Gordon just seemed to collapse on top of him.

Referee McCune blew a long blast on his whistle to indicate a serious foul. The usual finger-wagging followed before he pointed to somewhere, anywhere, off the pitch. 'The sin bin for you, laddie, for all of ten minutes,' he told Gordon. 'That was a terrible way to treat our guests, so it was. The wee laddie might have been buried alive!'

Gordon just grinned, wiped the sweat off his chest (he was one of several players on both sides to be bare-chested as team colours weren't necessary) and announced, 'Well, I could do wi' a rest.'

It took the 'wee laddie' quite a few moments to get to his feet. Jane, who'd stayed on the sidelines because she hadn't imagined Davey had really been hurt, now dashed across to help him to his feet. His hands were pressed against his lower abdomen and his face registered his pain.

'What's wrong, Davey?' she enquired gently as he remained almost bent double.

'Can't – get – my – breath,' he gasped.

She checked as far as she could but wasn't able to detect anything to worry her. 'I think you're just winded,' she said as he eased himself upright. 'Not surprised. That was a fearsome tackle.'

'How is the laddie?' Mr McCune enquired, looking genuinely concerned. 'Never thought

Gordon'd batter him like that. Not intentional, I'm sure.'

Davey managed to straighten up, blowing out his cheeks as if he'd just surfaced from beneath the nearby waves. 'If he *had* meant it I don't think I'd be alive!' he joked.

'Come on, let's get on with the game now they're a man short,' urged Larry, having sensed that Davey was going to be all right to resume playing in a moment.

'That's a bit calculating, Larry,' Jane said, smiling at the same time. 'But you're right!'

Davey, still massaging his stomach, stayed out on the flank until he felt better but it wasn't long before he was able to take another breather. For the Kings suffered a further setback, one that looked to Jane to be potentially worse than Davey's. In a frantic skirmish just on the edge of what was seen as the Kings' penalty area Josh and an opponent called Alisdair went down in a tangle of limbs. Then, as Alisdair got to his feet, he appeared to kick sand into Josh's face.

'Ouch!' yelled Josh, his hands scrabbling at his face. As Jane knew, he wore contact lenses. If he got sand behind them he would suffer a great deal of discomfort at the very least.

This time the ref didn't treat the incident as frivolous or trivial. When Jane informed him that Josh had lenses he took Alisdair to one side and it was plain to everyone that the lecture he gave him was severe. Then he held up his arm as if displaying a card and declared, 'You can all see that, can't you? And the colour is red. Which means you're sent off for the rest of the game. Anyone else who acts as stupidly as Ali will get the same. Don't tempt me to get mad again. Remember, this is supposed to be a bit of fun.'

It certainly didn't seem funny to Josh who was carefully using tissues provided by Jane to remove grains of sand from his eyes. His consolation was that the lenses were intact for it was his constant fear that he would lose or damage one during a game. As the stinging died away he told Jane, 'I'll be OK, Coach. Nothing to worry about.'

'Well done, Josh, you're always one of my bravest players,' she told him, and meant it. Josh was prepared to throw himself into dangerous situations, to go for fifty-fifty balls, that others might chicken out of at times. As she retreated to what made do as the touch-line Jane thought it was ironic that Josh had come unscathed through the last match on a rock-hard pitch, in spite of some tumbles, and yet here on sand he'd suffered. Fortunately, the sand-in-the-face was only a temporary hold-up in Josh's enthusiasm for playing an all-action game.

Davey, who'd now stopped rubbing his abdomen in favour of doing knees-up jumps on the spot, was swiftly back to his best with an oblique run across the entire width of the pitch, an example of ball control on a tricky surface that no one so far had matched. Then, just when it appeared he was intent on going all the way to score a brilliant solo goal, he back-heeled the ball to Reuben. And Reuben's accuracy with his left-foot was as good as usual, the ball being swept well wide of the keeper for the Kings' third goal.

'You're too good for us,' puffed Mr McCune who obviously wasn't half as fit as his players. 'You English are teaching us a thing or two today, Jane!'

'Well, you are two players down, aren't you, and we're just making the extra numbers count,' replied Jane, diplomatically not mentioning that it was entirely their own fault that Thistle had lost players. All the same, she was delighted with the Kings' performance on a strength-sapping surface. They'd had a long journey the previous evening and from what she'd gathered not everyone had slept well in their unfamiliar surroundings. Three of the squad had not previously spent a night away from home on their own; although they assured her they were enjoying themselves she had a few doubts.

She decided to give them another couple of minutes to round off their victory with perhaps another goal; she was aware how desperate Larry was to get on the score sheet but luck wasn't going his way. Somehow he wasn't nearly so effective on sand as he was on grass; he wasn't a natural dribbler and yet all the time he was trying to keep close control of the ball when he should have been just chasing after it. Lloyd was having similar problems so she decided to switch him into defence in place of Frazer who always enjoyed a storming run.

Lloyd gave her a rather wounded look

when she made the changes so she smiled and said, 'Don't worry, Lloyd, it probably won't be permanent!' In fact, it lasted barely a minute because, after Kieren was sent flying by a full-blooded shoulder charge, Mr McCune stopped the game to lecture his boys on their over-vigorous approach to a friendly wee match, as he put it. Jane took the opportunity to stroll over to her rival coach and say, 'Why don't we call it a day, Magnus? I think my boys at least are getting a bit weary. We also want to save some energy for tomorrow, you know. Oh yes, and I think the tide's getting closer!'

The stand-in ref glanced at the water-line and nodded. 'You're right there. I'm the local and I hadn't even noticed that. We'll stop now. I reckon you're making a shrewd move because you should always think of quitting when you're ahead! You're also right about conserving energy for Sunday morning. I'm sure we'll be trying hard to take our revenge then. At the moment it's Scotland o England 1, isn't it? We'll strive to level things off.'

'I know you will, Magnus, but usually we play very well away from home – and maybe the further we are away from home the better we'll play,' she smiled. 'Anyway, it's time I rounded up my boys and made sure they're not in danger of catching a chill. I think it's getting a bit cooler, probably because the tide's on the turn. Don't want anyone missing tonight's party.'

'Aye, I'm sure you're right about the weather. See you tonight then. I'll try to make sure my laddies are a wee bit more hospitable than they were at beach soccer!'

The Kings were perfectly content with the hospitality of the people they were staying with and Lloyd was ecstatic about the meals he'd eaten. 'They're vegetarians, the folk I'm with, and the nut roast we had for tea was out of this world!' he told Jane when the squad began to arrive at the youth centre where the evening entertainment to be provided ranged from video games to pool and a mini-basketball tournament. 'Guess what? Mrs Donald is going to give me the recipe so I can get my mum to make it for us!'

'Did you get porridge this morning?' enquired Oats. 'It's the real stuff here.'

'Definitely – and that's great, too. Don't

know why you ever wanted to leave Scotland, Oats. It's a great place.'

'I second that,' contributed Reuben, who had just joined them. 'This place is really peaceful. Didn't know houses could be so quiet. At home it's a madhouse most of the time.'

'Well, I was sorry to leave when we had to move to Rodale Kings,' Frazer reminisced. 'But if we hadn't I wouldn't have met you guys and started to play for the Goal Kings. And that's the best thing that's happened in my football life. Well, until I play for Scotland. You never know, one day I might be playing for my country in the blue shirt against some of you lot in the white shirts of England!'

'Or whatever colour I choose for the England goalkeeper's jersey!' Danny grinned.

It was the pool table that captivated Lloyd and he proved to be such a good potter that it was difficult for any of his team-mates to get the cue out of his hand when they wanted to play. But then he was in demand to play in two-man teams against the Thistle boys so he couldn't have been happier.

Josh was enjoying himself, too, because his

height was ideal for the basketball games though he always kept an eye on Alisdair, the freckle-faced boy who'd brought him down on the beach. The sand had soon been removed and, of course, there wasn't any on the youth club floor. Josh, however, was ready to deal with any other form of illegal tackle.

Frazer somehow felt left out of things. It was strange to be again among so many people with Scottish accents. Yet he didn't any longer feel to be one of them, just as he wasn't, on this occasion, truly one of the visitors. He felt to be in a kind of no-man's land. To his surprise, he found himself wishing that Andrea were here. Because they were fairly close in age they always spent a lot of time together, swimming and playing tennis and doing their football training. He could play just as hard against her as any boy and she never complained about bruises or minor injuries (well, not until the other day). He thought she was just as tough as he was. Now, though, he'd just be happy to stroll along the beach with her, jumping away from waves, just having fun and talking about their school friends in Scotland and the things that had happened to them when they lived here.

He was still in that mood when he noticed Danny edging towards the exit and then disappearing. What was he up to? Frazer decided to follow him and didn't think anyone would notice his departure. After the mildness of the day the temperature had dropped and rain was falling lightly from an overcast sky, and it was much darker than Frazer expected it to be. Danny had already crossed the forecourt and was heading for a sheltered seat on a raised area of ground overlooking the promenade. Frazer, taking cover behind bushes and trees in case the Kings' skipper looked round, was intrigued when he saw Danny drop on to one of the seats facing the sea and then hunch forward as if trying to get warm. Surely it wasn't cold enough for that? And what on earth had prompted him to come out here all on his own?

Frazer, motionless now about fifty metres away from his team-mate, tried to imagine a reason. Was he meeting someone, a girl perhaps who lived locally? Hardly likely: there hadn't been an opportunity for socializing beyond being polite to the host families.

Oh, unless there was a girl in the house where Danny was staying and *she* was the one he was waiting for. Then it occurred to him that perhaps the team's captain was going to have a secret meeting with the coach, a meeting they didn't want the Aberlyn Thistle people to know about because it would focus on plans for tomorrow's version of Scotland v England. Frazer remembered that Mrs Allenby hadn't been among the crowd just now in the club room so perhaps she was making her way to this secret rendezvous with the captain. Instinctively, Frazer glanced round but could see nothing to confirm that suspicion. But perhaps the likeliest solution to the mystery was the simplest: Danny just wanted to be on his own. He might be homesick and couldn't bear being with lots of people who were enjoying themselves. Frazer could sympathize with that: in spite of being back in his native Scotland at this minute he was actually missing his family and Rodale Kings.

Suddenly Danny stood up, snapped his hands together in a curious way and turned towards Frazer. And in that instant Frazer realized what Danny had done: he'd closed down the aerial of a mobile phone. He'd been making, or taking, a private phone call!

'Hey, Oats, what're you doing? Not spying on me, are you?' Danny challenged him.

'Course not! Just need some fresh air. Bit stuffy in there, isn't it? And then, well, just say you and – and –'

'I was trying to get hold of Sophie,' Danny announced, not really caring about Frazer's explanation. 'She should've been there, promised she would be. But she isn't, her mum says. So what's she up to?'

'Sophie? Oh, is she your girl-friend in Rodale?' Frazer enquired innocently.

'She's supposed to be but sometimes I wonder, Oats, I really do,' was the rather bitter response. 'She won't *admit* she's my girl-friend, says that's too *definite*, whatever that's supposed to mean. But when we *are* together, just on our own, well, she's *definitely* a girl and she's definitely friendly! But if I'm with some of the guys or we're just talking on the phone then she doesn't want to know. Weird, really.'

'Did her mum give you any idea where she might be?' enquired Oats, intrigued by this news of Danny's relationship. 'D'you think she's covering up for her? Or – yes, maybe she doesn't want you going out with her daughter and so she's, well, protecting her.'

Danny shook his head. 'Don't think she minds that I'm dating her daughter. Sophie's definitely been out with other guys so it's nothing new to her mum. Honestly, I don't think Mrs Crosland has a clue where Sophie is at this very minute. Wish *I* did.'

By unspoken, common consent they'd walked back to where Danny had been sitting in the shelter and now he slumped down on the seat, legs stretched out in front of him, staring at the darkness of the sea. Frazer couldn't really empathize with him because of his own lack of experience in the matter of girl-friends but he was keen to hear other details if Danny could bear to relate them.

'Does you own mum know about Sophie? What does she think about her when –'

'Haven't got a mum,' Danny interrupted sharply. 'Well, I mean I have biologically but she left us a couple of years ago. She doesn't come into my life so that's no problem.'

'Oh, sorry, didn't know about that, Dan. So what about your dad, then?'

'He's OK, lets me get on with my life, really. Even lent me his mobile for this trip, just for emergencies, he said. But trying to get in touch with a missing girl-friend *is* an emergency, isn't it?' There was a change in his voice as his normal good humour returned. 'Listen, what about you, Oats? Have you got a girl in your life?'

'Er no, not yet. I mean, I'm interested but it hasn't happened. You know, I haven't seen the right one anywhere.' He paused and then for some reason he would have found hard to explain, added, 'My sister says I don't even notice other girls but she's wrong there.'

'Didn't know you'd got a sister,' said Danny, his interest quickening. 'What's she like?'

'Well, she's a year younger than me but everybody seems to think she looks older,' Frazer revealed. 'But she's not a bit like Sophie. In looks, I mean. I –'

'How d'you know that, Oats?' Danny demanded, suspicious.

'Well, I've seen her, of course, with you – or, sort of *nearly* with you when Josh and I found you waiting for her in Candle Park.'

'Oh, right. I'd forgotten you were there.

Sorry. Go on about your sister – what's she called?'

'Andrea, though I often just call her Andi. Think she likes that. She's tall and pretty thin and, oh yes, she's got blonde hair that's in a ponytail. Actually, she turned up at our match with Friday Bridge. She was with my mum and they were talking to Mrs Allenby for a bit. They –'

'Oh, I remember!' Danny cut in. 'Yeah, the one with the blonde ponytail. Remember her! Didn't know she was your *sister*, Oats.'

'Well, she doesn't let me forget it, that's the truth. She's mad on football herself and we train together quite a bit. She's got a kick like a – a mule when she wants to use it. I know, I've had the bruises to prove it! I'll give her this, though, she doesn't whinge too much if I kick her. Says a kick is all part of the game. She asked about you, Dan.'

'You serious?'

'Aye, she did, honest,' replied Frazer before suddenly realizing it might be wise not to say too much in case any part of this conversation got back to Andrea, though he couldn't think how that would be possible. 'I think it was just that she was surprised that any of us had a girl-friend.'

'You told her about Sophie?'

'Well no, not really. Just said that you knew a girl called Sophie. Er, look, Danny, think I'd better get back to the youth club. Maybe there'll be a chance of a game of pool if anybody's been able to prise that cue out of Lloyd's grasp. Coming?'

'In a minute, maybe. Just give Sophie a quick ring, see if she's back home yet. Hope so. Oh, and thanks for telling me about Andrea, Oats. Nice to know *one* girl is interested in me.'

6 In the Mist

Davey peered at the figures on the other side of the pitch and said to no one in particular, 'Those guys look even bigger today. Don't think most of them are the ones we played on the beach yesterday.'

Josh, who'd been rubbing his eyes because of a minor problem with the lenses, said, 'Don't know how you can see through all this fog. Probably be too bad for us even to start this match.'

'No, nothing like that,' declared Dominic. 'Mum's been in touch with some local weather expert and he says it'll clear within the hour. Mum's decided that we should play up the slope in the first half because this mist – that's what it is, Josh, Scottish mist, not fog – the mist'll linger at the top end. Also we'll be playing downhill in the second half when maybe we'll have less energy.'

'Oh,' said Josh, impressed with this unexpectedly detailed meteorological report. 'Hope she's right. Just as long as that lot don't steam-roller us in the first half.'

'I really like the way your mum takes the trouble to work things out like that,' Reuben remarked. 'Shows she thinks of everything, not just the sort of tactics we should use. I haven't met a coach like her before and I've played for a few teams.'

'You're right, Lefty,' enthused Danny, who felt it was time the captain joined in this chat. He was feeling in a particularly good mood this morning since managing a sixty-five second conversation with Sophie immediately after his early breakfast and before she had left her house to sing in a choir. In spite of the brevity of the call it had been wonderful to hear her voice. That alone was going to inspire his game this morning, he told himself. 'If our previous coach had seen this fog – sorry, Dom, mist – and that slope he'd've just told us to ignore 'em. He wouldn't have worked out how they might help us.'

'You're right, skipper,' replied Reuben who still wasn't quite sure that he liked being called

Lefty, although he thought on balance he probably did. Danny had minted the name on the journey north because, he claimed, he'd recently seen an old movie in which there was a gangster called Lefty who really did look a bit like Reuben. Moreover, Reuben was famed for being brilliantly left-footed, so it all fitted. Reuben was grateful to Jane for not trying to persuade him, as all his previous coaches had done, to make more use of his right foot. Gradually he was beginning to do just that and he suspected his all-round game was improving as a result.

'Tell you who ought to be here today – Foggy,' said Larry Hill as the players changed into their playing kit in the impressive dressing-room of a modern clubhouse. 'I mean, it lives up to his name and we might need a foghorn to warn us what's in front of us!'

Most of them laughed and Larry smirked; he believed he was now an established member of the team and he wanted the rest of the players to recognize that as a fact. From time to time it still troubled him to remember the teachers who'd said of him that he looked 'too soft to be a striker'. In every match he played he wanted to prove how tough he could be while still scoring unforgettable goals.

When Jane Allenby came in, casting admiring glances at the facilities the changing-room offered, the boys were still laughing at an anecdote Lloyd was telling about the gargantuan breakfast he'd eaten and the kindness of his hosts in saying he could take as much of the fruit as he wanted to share with his team-mates after the match or on the trip home. 'When I saw how many apples they were giving me for you guys I just said, "Cor!" You get that, don't you?'

'Well, I was going to tell you that the important thing about this game is that you should just go out and enjoy it,' she announced when the jokes at last died down. 'But you seem to have started your enjoyment already. Good to hear that you're in such a merry mood. I know that lots of managers are supposed to tell their teams to "go and enjoy yourselves" when it's kick-off time. Today we're here for the fun of it. That was the idea for the entire weekend. Has anybody *not* enjoyed it so far?'

The chorus of 'nos' and 'it's been greats!' was the response she'd hoped for and it was good to see that Dominic was joining in. Deliberately she hadn't let herself be too close to him throughout the weekend and yet it seemed to her that their coach-player relationship was beginning to match their easy-going mother-and-son companionship.

'Excellent! So you'll just play your normal game and we'll hope the mist clears quickly so that the spectators can enjoy your style. One thing to mention: I don't think it'll turn out to be as easy for you as the beach soccer. Mr McCune tells me that a few of yesterday's players can't make it today so he's had to draft in some replacements. But he promises they're of the same standard as the boys you trounced on the beach. So –'

'But that's just what I said when we spotted them before we came in here,' Davey burst out. 'The new ones are a lot bigger than the others. Must be older, I reckon.'

'Oh, that's interesting,' she replied. 'Didn't know about that. Still, it won't really matter. After all, this is just a friendly game.'

'Didn't feel very friendly on the beach,' Davey muttered darkly.

'Oh, Davey, I'm sorry! I didn't ask: how're you feeling today? No problems still after being flattened, I hope.'

'Well, it's still a bit sore down there. But it'll go soon, I expect.'

'Oh good,' she said, relieved. 'You were very brave about it, Davey. And Josh, you also. Any problems with your eyes?'

'Just can't see how to score goals when he plays at the back!' joked Lloyd, who'd been waiting to make a crack like that; and it duly won him a few laughs.

'I can see everything I need to see,' replied Josh rather formally as he shot a scowl at Lloyd. 'I've already checked and there's no sand on the pitch out there.'

Jane nodded. 'Good. Right, it's time to move. Don't forget, Danny, if you win the toss, choose uphill. I'm sure it'll pay off. OK, let the Kings rule!'

Danny duly won the toss, chose which way to face, plainly to the surprise of his opposing captain, and thus everything looked as if it would go according to plan. In reality, nothing else went right for the Kings for a long time. Aberlyn Thistle wore black and gold stripes which made many people immediately think of wasps; and the team buzzed and flitted and quite quickly stung like angry wasps. Their first attack was literally launched from the kick-off when they swarmed down the slope in numbers before the Kings could manage so much as a solitary touch of the ball. The bulk and weight of the raiding forwards was very different from what Jane had seen the previous day and she sensed within minutes that she had made a serious miscalculation.

The only reason Thistle didn't score in their initial attack was because Joe Parbold was adjudged to have been fouled by his opponent after the Kings' central defender tried a fairly desperate sliding tackle to win the ball. The Aberlyn player thought he was losing possession when Joe's outstretched leg just failed to reach the ball; and so he turned sharply and shoved Joe to the ground before racing on. It was the ref's whistle that brought him back. The culprit started to remonstrate with him until the ref told him, 'Say another word, son, and ye're booked, that ye are!' Sensibly, the boy shut up.

The free kick brought only temporary relief. Although Davey jumped high to try to reach the ball his huge opponent, Thistle's sweeper, headed it down nonchalantly for a team-mate to feed their right-winger. From the flank, a splendidly slick passing movement took the ball into the Kings' penalty area; and none of the visiting players got much more than a toe-end to it before Thistle's burly centre-forward rammed it past Danny with dismaying ease. The Scots celebrated in a fairly restrained manner as if they were simply doing only what was expected of them; they gave the impression they knew they'd be doing it again very soon.

That confidence wasn't misplaced. Within five minutes they were charging down the slope again like warriors bent on destroying foreign raiders. Frazer, who'd tried to make a raid of his own down the left flank before losing the ball, was by-passed as a leggy winger made the most of the space left to him. The Kings' defence was spread wide when the cross came over. For once Josh was out-jumped in going for the ball and no one else could prevent the muscular Thistle striker from trying a snap shot from close range. His aim was perfect. Danny hadn't a chance of reaching the ball as it entered the net at the point where the upright met the crossbar.

Jane gulped. Two-down in hardly any time at all when she'd been expecting her Kings to inflict that sort of score on the opposition! From the way Aberlyn were playing it wasn't just the slope that was in their favour. In complete contrast to the 'fun' game on the beach they were moving the ball about with speed and precision and, above all, purpose. They knew exactly what they were doing – and were doing it superbly, that had to be admitted. Her problem was to find a way, if there *was* a way, of stemming the tide of their attacks.

It wasn't difficult to make the first decision. As Frazer retreated into his own half to take up a position for the restart she called, 'Frazer, stay back from now on. We've got to defend in depth. Don't leave gaps.' He acknowledged her instructions but couldn't help wondering if he personally was being held to blame for the scoreline. After all, both goal-bearing attacks had started on the right, *his* flank. That thought didn't help his play when Thistle burst in the Kings' half again. Only a bad bounce of the ball and an unlucky ricochet from a team-mate's shin prevented the winger from making deadly progress again.

As soon as she could catch the ear of one of her players Jane delivered another urgent message. 'Tell Reuben to keep possession as long as possible. You've all got to work like mad to *keep* the ball. Hang on to it at all costs. Slow the game down.'

She doubted that would really work because it was plain that Thistle were by far the bigger and stronger players and sometimes that strength simply overwhelmed opponents who were slighter in build. Davey wasn't one of them because his strength was in his legs and he was very difficult to dispossess in spite of his lack of height. Sensing the need to reinforce the midfield he'd already dropped back, allowing Larry to play the role of lone striker. The way things were going at present, the Kings wouldn't be doing much attacking, anyway.

While Jane was reviewing her options

Magnus McCune came strolling along the touchline doing nothing to disguise his pleasure in the way the game was going. 'Well, I think we may be getting our revenge today, Jane,' he greeted her. 'Didna like losing yesterday, ye know.'

Jane wasn't used to coaches who came to gloat before a match was even half over; or at any time, come to that. So she responded with just what was in her mind. 'I'm not sure I recognize some of your players. Somehow, they seem different from those we played on the beach.'

'Oh aye, that's so in just a couple of cases,' Magnus admitted casually. 'The ones missing were needed for the choir so I just brought in some reserves, giving them a run out to see what they're capable of and – oh, great run, Jamie, laddie, great – GOAL!'

Jane swung back to the game just in time to see the net bulge behind Danny who was flat on the ground. Her defence looked transfixed, almost dazed, by what was happening. This assault down the slope was fiercer than anything they'd experienced before anywhere. But then, it had long ago occurred to some of the Kings that they were up against boys quite a bit older than themselves, players who almost certainly were regularly playing in a grade of football much higher than the Highlea Junior Sunday League.

'If this were a game of cricket I think I'd be asking you if you were going to declare your first innings closed,' she said with grim humour.

'Och no, we'd not declare in any game,' replied the unamused Mr McCune. 'A challenge match is a challenge match and must be fought to the finish, Jane. Remember what I said about yesterday's result. It has to be avenged.'

After that, there was nothing more to be said and Jane deliberately moved away on the pretence of wanting to transmit a message to Lloyd. She needed him to move into the middle and help the battered midfield because he was serving no purpose on the right wing. Her worry was that if the defeat was very heavy then it could well undermine the confidence the Kings had just come to feel in their own abilities as a unit. Psychologically, it would be damaging. And defeat was all that could be contemplated; at present the only uncertainty was how large the half-time score would be. The cricket quip might easily rebound on her if that score reached double figures.

Then a factor she hadn't imagined existed came into play in her favour. The Thistles became *over*-confident. They started making elementary mistakes, hitting passes that were too far in front of a team-mate or went to an opponent. They called for the ball and then failed to control it. They thought all they had to do to outwit a challenger was to run up to him and swerve one way or the other before going past him. The Kings, however, were obeying Jane's constant dictum in training sessions: never take your eye off the ball. So the tacklers in purple and white were at last beginning to draw the sting from the black and yellow raiders. Danny, true to his promises, was forever yelling encouragement to his team-mates and Lloyd, too, had started to praise a good tackle or a neat interception. Much as the bouncy, curly-haired winger enjoyed going forward he seemed to be just as motivated when battling for possession in midfield. Jane was heartened by that and some of the other qualities being displayed by her team. If they could keep playing like this then all might not be lost in spite of the 0–3 scoreline.

Unfortunately, the spell without a goal being scored ended before half-time. Just when Jane was coming to believe that the worst might be over the Thistle attackers rediscovered their touch, got their act together and once more swept down on the visitors in awesome strength. Josh, who'd played valiantly until that point and scarcely made so much as a semblance of a mistake, suddenly lost his composure. As Alisdair came at him with the ball at his feet Josh went in with a two-footed tackle that was almost a jump. Alisdair had parted with the ball just a split-second earlier and was unprepared for this particular assault. Still, he made the most of it when, unhurt, he scrambled to his feet.

'Penalty!' he roared. 'Come on, ref, ye've got to give it, man!'

And, despite looking a trifle apologetic, the ref reacted by pointing with dramatic emphasis right at the spot.

'Oh no, couldn't be! Wasn't even in the box!'
Josh wailed. But when he looked round he
saw that he was wrong. He'd caught Alisdair
just on the wrong side of the line. The Scot, of
course, was ecstatic at getting what he wanted.
Josh regarded him with loathing. For the
boy who'd kicked sand in his face had now
managed to inflict punishment on the entire
team.

For, as seemed inevitable, the penalty-taker
drove the ball high into the right-hand side of
the net with even the agile Danny unable to
get so much as a fingertip to it. At least
the Thistle celebrations were restrained,
possibly because they were convinced now
they'd exacted revenge for their humiliation
on the beach.

'If they go on like this they'll hit us for a
cricket score,' Josh moaned to Kieren as they
awaited the resumption. 'Hope they declare
when they've got enough!'

Kieren grinned. 'It won't be as bad as that.
Remember, *we* are playing down the slope in
the second half. Then we'll start scoring, just
as long as the strikers are in form.'

The Kings understandably looked downcast

as they trooped off for the interval with the score still 0–4. 'Don't look so worried,' Jane greeted them, deliberately cheerful. 'You've fought well against a bigger, *much* bigger, and stronger team. You could easily have conceded almost double figures, a cricket score!'

Josh shot a triumphant glance at Kieren, thrilled that he and their coach had used practically the same metaphor. But Kieren was munching a chocolate bar supplied by his dad. Clark Kelly knew that out of loyalty he ought to have been supporting Jane but the present score, he felt, was an embarrassment. This trip to Scotland, he now believed, had been a mistake; the Kings would travel home, a long journey, probably remembering only a heavy defeat. Well, Kieren would.

'You don't think we've played badly, then, Coach?' enquired Reuben.

She shook her head vigorously. 'Considering the opposition, as I've just said, I think you've done very well indeed to hold them to four goals, one of which was a penalty. In the second half the slope will be in your favour and I really believe if we can get an early goal we can still win. Or, at worst, lose only narrowly. So there's still a lot to play for. And, remember, boys, this is a *fun* game. We're not losing out on League points. So that's why the result doesn't matter a jot. Next week is when we need to win again. That's when we get down to the really serious business of climbing the League.'

Clark Kelly, who overheard that, was sure this was the wrong attitude but he wasn't going to enter into a dispute in public. During the first half he'd been hoping, as Thistle grew ever more dominant, that the mist would thicken and cause an abandonment. The reverse had happened. Now the sun was shining through as visibility improved and conditions would only get better. He consoled himself with the thought that at least the long drive home in the minibus should be in good weather.

The incline did appear to work in the Kings' favour because, five minutes into the second half, Reuben, picking up a sweetly-struck pass from Lloyd, accelerated past an all too casual defender and darted into the box. Larry, homing in from the opposite corner, screamed for the ball. But Reuben sensed this might be the best chance he'd ever have of scoring a goal in Scotland. His pace barely slackened as he turned another defender with a delightful sleight-of-the-foot and then, as calmly as if he were on a training pitch, he lifted the ball over the goalkeeper's head and into the back of the net.

Even Magnus McCune joined in the ringing applause for what was easily the best goal so far. Larry Hill, however, wasn't pleased and Jane could hear his complaint, 'I'd've scored if only you'd passed to me, Lefty. I was in a better position and I *am* a striker. But you haven't given me a pass all morning!' Reuben, however, was too happy to do more than grin at his scowling team-mate.

Jane wasn't pleased with Larry's complaint. If he was going to continue in that vein then he might easily become another Foggy, and that was an unhappy prospect. So when Larry was near enough a few minutes later she called just loud enough for him to hear, 'Larry, it doesn't matter *who* scores for us as long as somebody does. This is a *team* game.' The striker with the strangely flat hairstyle gave her a startled look but didn't say anything; well, nothing she heard. In fact, Larry was quite pleased she'd listened to his remark to Lefty because it would show her how ambitious he was as a goal-scorer. In his view, if you didn't want to score every goal for your side then you ought not to be playing.

Aberlyn were determined not to be out-shone in the matter of hitting the best individual goal of the game and within ten minutes had added two more goals to their tally as a result of surging raids through the middle of the Kings' defence where Joe and Kieren were overpowered by the physical strength of their opponents. Danny heroically got in the way of one power drive but was helpless to prevent the ball being flicked into the net when the shooter followed up; and then the goalkeeper couldn't get within a metre of a towering header from a central defender who'd moved up for a corner kick.

'Don't let it get to seven!' prayed Jane to her personal sporting saviour. 'Six is bad enough but seven seems so *crushing*.'

That plea was not only answered in her favour but, with just a minute left, the Kings were awarded a penalty for what the ref signalled was a handling offence right on the edge of the box. Jane hadn't seen anything amiss and nor had anyone else apart from the official but although the Thistle players combined in a ritualistic protest the kick had to be taken. Jane suspected the ref was simply trying to provide the Kings with a kinder scoreline and a better note on which to end their first game in Scotland, a game against bigger and stronger opposition.

Once again Davey seized the ball for the last chance he was going to get to put his name on the score-sheet, just supposing such a sheet existed for a 'friendly'. He knew exactly where he was going to hit his shot and that's where it went, raging into the top right-hand corner of the net with the goalkeeper well beaten. After the hammering they'd taken, his team-mates still had just enough energy left to fall on Davey with congratulatory hugs, much to his delight. He knew he could never get too much praise for goal-scoring.

Danny was still thinking about the Kings' goals when the long journey home began because he was sitting with Reuben and

Davey. 'At least you guys've got something good to remember about that game. But I let in six. Total disaster!'

'Something good might've happened to me,' said Frazer, sitting on the other side of the minibus. 'I heard this guy on the touch-line say to his pal, "That boy can play a wee bit." I know he meant me because I'd just gone on that fast run down the wing and got in a great cross. Pity no one got on the end of it. Anyway, I also heard the ref say there was a Scotland selector present. So that could've been him!'

'Great!' Danny murmured without much feeling. 'Listen, can't wait to get home and see Sophie. She says she'll be waiting for me! How about that, fellas?'

'Wish I had a girl-friend waiting for me,' remarked Reuben. 'All I've got is family, family, family.'

'I know just how you feel,' said Davey. 'I've only got one sister but she's a lot of pain. Always in the bathroom when I want to be there or watching TV when I want to see a different channel. You'd be doing me a favour, Lefty, if you could get her out of our house for a bit.'

'Oh, really,' said Reuben, eyes brightening. 'When do I get to meet her, Davey?'

'Not sure about that but my mum says she's coming to watch us one day soon so I'll try to get her to bring Katie along, too. *If* Mum can get her out of the bathroom in time!'

While the boys were contentedly discussing their present and future social life Jane, at the front of the bus, was still brooding on the defeat. 'I made a mistake, I must admit it,' she confessed to Clark Kelly who was at the wheel. 'I should never have fixed up something as risky as this. You know, without being really aware of the opposition.'

'We were ripped off, that's the truth,' Kieren's father declared. 'Some of their lads must have been at least two years older than ours. And twice the size! I just hope we learn something from it, that's all.'

'It's the size of the defeat that worries me,' admitted Jane. 'It's likely to prey on their minds. How long are the Kings going to take to get over it?'

7 *Counter-attacks*

At a brisk pace Frazer turned into Prince's Close and was just about to hurry up the short drive to Danny's home when he stopped dead. For the up-and-over garage door was open and there stood Danny, punching two-fistedly at a bag slung from the ceiling and occupying the space where the car would normally be. Danny was wearing scarlet boxing gloves and just a T-shirt and football shorts. So intent was he on his hitting that he didn't seem aware of his team-mate's arrival until Frazer spoke.

'Hey, who's your enemy, Danny? Looks like you're going to kill him! Didn't know you went in for boxing.'

'I *would* murder him if he were here,' was the forceful response. 'Lad called Leon. Stupid name. Been sneaking off with Sophie behind my back. You know, when we've been training and times like that.'

Frazer wasn't sure how to respond to that. After all, this Leon could hardly have been dating Sophie if she hadn't wanted to be with him. Still, he supposed Danny had worked that out for himself but couldn't admit that Sophie herself might be to blame. So he pointed to the swinging punchbag.

'How long have you had that and the gloves? I mean, are you really taking up boxing?'

Danny shook his head and wiped sweat away from his grey eyes with the back of his wrist. 'Just a way of strengthening my arms and shoulders. Goalies need to be able to punch properly, you know. You saw what happened when I made a mess of that cross against Tolworth. Gave 'em their goal on a plate when the ball went straight to their striker. It's not going to happen again, Oats. Next time I'll punch the ball all the way to the centre circle!'

'That's fighting talk,' grinned Frazer, pleased with the pun even if Danny didn't recognize it. 'Anyway, that goal didn't matter, did it, because we still cruised past 'em. Four-one's a fair score against a team that was level with us in the table till then. Just hope we're in the same form today against Stonecreek Pirates. If we thrash them we'll be in the top four! I fancy that.'

'Don't think Reuben does. He used to play for the Pirates and he's worried some of his old mates will be gunning for him. A lot of them didn't like him just because he was easily their best player and I think he told 'em they'd be useless without him!'

'Well, you'll have to protect him, Dan. If you keep your gloves handy – get it?! – you'll be able to knock 'em all out. Hey, listen, if you don't get a move on we'll never make the kick-off. It's after ten already.'

'Really? OK, come up with me while I get changed. Won't take a minute.'

While Danny stripped off his kit and vigorously towelled himself down Frazer prowled round his team-mate's bedroom, somewhere he'd never been before, admiring the sporting trophies and a variety of photos of Danny himself and his dad. One picture in particular held his attention: that of a remarkably pretty girl with long, chestnut hair and holding a badminton racket.

'I see you've still got a picture of Sophie on

display,' he remarked while still wondering whether it was wise to talk about her; but then, he really wanted to know more about her.

Danny, rummaging in a drawer for a fresh pair of shorts at last found what he was looking for and turned round. 'Yeah, well, I *am* still dating her, until I find somebody else. Hey, didn't you say you'd got a sister who was asking about me? Andrea, isn't it?'

'Aye, that's right. She says she might come to another match soon. Still hoping to get into a boys' team if she can. I'll introduce you if I get the chance.' His pause was fractional before he touched on what really interested him. 'Dan, d'you know if any of the other Kings have got a sister – sisters, maybe?'

'I expect so. Reuben, definitely. He's got loads of sisters, and brothers, all younger than him.' Danny was now admiring his new scarlet-and-black goalkeeper's shirt in the mirror before putting on his tracksuit for the short journey to the football ground. 'Oh yeah, Davey was talking about his sister on the way back from Scotland. Says she's a pain, though. And Josh has mentioned his sister, Chrissie I think her name is. She plays tennis, like

Sophie. So that's a few to be going on with, Oats.'

'Oh, right,' Frazer murmured, deciding he'd learned as much as he needed at this stage. He couldn't, though, resist a last glance at the lovely Sophie before they left.

The only thing on Marc Thrale's mind when the squad assembled before the match was his place on the bench; his fury at not being picked to start the game was boiling over. 'You *need* me there, Coach,' he claimed. 'We're not scoring goals and we're messing things up in midfield.'

Jane had heard this sort of complaint from him so many times she'd almost given up listening. She was well aware that he had skills he could contribute to the Kings but at present she had a settled team that was doing all, or nearly all, she asked of it. All the same, she didn't want to disappoint Foggy to the extent that he would 'do an Alex', as Dominic had put it, and walk out on the squad. They hadn't so many spare players they could do without him completely; and, moreover, his energy and enthusiasm when he did get on the pitch were definite assets.

'Marc, when the time is right I'll put you on,' she said quietly in a corner of the dressing-room, though keeping her voice down hardly mattered when Foggy himself practically shouted every word he uttered. 'I don't think we can be doing so badly when we've dropped only one point in six matches since the Scottish trip. So –'

'Yeah, but look what happened in Scotland when I wasn't there. You got thrashed!'

She sighed. 'Marc, if you mean *us*, well, we did lose heavily. But we also scored two goals against a really tough team. That turned out to be success, not failure. The Kings have built on it since. Team spirit is wonderful. The Scottish experience did us a lot of good. It's a pity you couldn't share in it.'

'Wasn't my fault I couldn't go that week-end!' he interrupted. 'But I'm being blamed for not being there. I know I am. That's why I'm always a sub!'

'Marc, I've told you: I've picked the team for this game on the basis of recent performances. You're on the bench to start with. If I can put you on, I will. Now, try to think about the team, not just yourself. I've got plenty of other things to consider.'

One problem she hadn't expected involved the referee. It was a couple of minutes into the game before she realized how much his black and yellow top clashed with the Pirates' navy blue and yellow quartered shirts. In fact, it was only when Reuben went down under a scything tackle from an opponent and she looked for the referee's reactions: for a few moments she couldn't even spot him. Then, belatedly, he noticed something was wrong and signalled for her to come on to attend to the injured player.

As she dashed across the pitch Jane wondered whether she ought to tell the little man – and he *was* shorter than several of the players – that he ought to change his shirt. But would he resent her 'interference' and so look unfavourably on the Kings? That was certainly a risk and she didn't know whether to take it. After all, the Pirates' coach hadn't raised any objection, so far as she knew.

Reuben was grimacing and clutching his ankle. 'Knew they'd get me as soon as they could,' he muttered, shooting fierce glances at a huddle of his former team-mates. 'That was Ricky Wade who did this, Ricky the Wrecker we used to call him. But I'll get my own back and –'

'No, Reuben!' she told him as she checked the extent of the damage. 'We're not going to have any retaliation, any trouble. It's the ref's job to sort out offenders. Just keep cool. I don't want to make any substitutions, OK?'

He had the sense to nod and she patted his leg after applying analgesic spray. 'No damage done. You'll be fine.'

After helping him to his feet she smiled at the ref and motioned that she'd like a word with him in private, so they moved a few steps to one side. 'Hope you don't mind my saying this, ref, but did you realize your shirt colours are almost identical to Stonecreek's?'

'Oh, really,' he replied, looking round in genuine surprise. 'Well, Coach, I think you're right. Well spotted. I carry a spare shirt so I'll nip over and change.'

Relieved at that reaction she took the plunge and mentioned another matter as they hurried across the pitch together. 'Please don't think I'm trying to influence any decisions you make, ref, but I think you should know that the boy who's just been injured used to play for the Pirates. I'm sure there isn't a vendetta or anything like that but I know he fears his old team-mates may, er, be a bit rough with him. No reason for it but, well, that's the way some players are, isn't it?'

He nodded. 'I'll bear it in mind, Coach. Happens all the time, actually, so I know how to deal with it.'

The Stonecreek coach shot an enquiring look at both of them but it was to a companion that he voiced his opinion, 'Obviously doing her best to influence the ref to see things her way. Well, he won't be able to cancel out all the goals we're going to score!'

As it turned out, his confidence wasn't misplaced because within five minutes the fastest and most lethal of the Pirates sliced through the heart of the Kings' defence, exchanged a clever one-two with their leading striker and calmly planted the ball into the net as Danny dived just too late at his feet.

'I'd never have let him get through that gap, wide as a runway it was. I'd've closed him down on the halfway line,' declared Foggy, conveniently forgetting that he always claimed he was a forward, not a defender.

Jane, attempting to plan a counter-attack, found it easy to ignore her vocal sub at that point but only a few minutes later she needed him: Reuben went down under another reckless assault and this time he clearly wasn't fit to continue although she couldn't detect any real damage to his ankle. At least, this time, the offender was duly punished with a yellow card and a very public warning about his fate if he transgressed again.

'You're on, Marc,' she told him. 'But I want you on the left of midfield, remember. And if Frazer makes a run to the box, drop back, cover the gap. Just play to orders, OK? We've got to hold things together while the Pirates are in this mood.'

Foggy had his track suit off before Jane finished speaking and, rejoicing with air-punching gestures, he raced on to the pitch; then he turned to wave to somebody on the opposite touch-line and stuck a thumb high in the air. Within moments he was in the midst of the action, picking up a misguided pass by an opponent and hurtling forward to set up an attack with an astute flick in Davey's direction. Davey tricked an opponent with an equally smart feint before whipping over a cross for Larry to try a shot on goal. Unhappily Larry's aim was woeful and the ball ballooned over the bar.

'Pity, that – a great move started by Foggy just wasted!' someone in the crowd sang out loudly enough for most people to hear. Jane, attending still to Reuben whose ankle was now packed round with icebags, barely heard what was being said; her mind was on how the Kings were going to get back into the match. Soon, however, other remarks in praise of Foggy's play from the same source reached her. 'Oh, great shot, Foggy – oh, really unlucky not to score!' and, 'Brilliant pass, Foggy, just brilliant!' were typical examples. Jane at last identified the spectator. He was too young to be Foggy's dad but she supposed he could be an older brother. The Thrales were not a family she'd had anything to do with and Foggy himself rarely spoke about them so she had no way of knowing who was so publicly extolling his play. Most of it was deserved because, as she could see now, he really was playing well. Perhaps she had been at fault in keeping him on the bench for such a run of matches, even though the Kings had been winning without his help.

In spite of Foggy's promptings the Kings were not looking like winners in this game and a hesitant Joe Parbold almost allowed the Pirates to snatch another goal right on half-time. Only a fingertip save from Danny kept the ball out of the net.

Jane considered taking Joe off and replacing him with Gareth Kingstree for the second half but decided against such a move until later in case there were more injuries. Larry for one had taken a knock when brought down in full flight, which was another booking for a Pirate, and Kieren was limping, though he insisted he was fine when the coach asked if anything was wrong. After recent snowfalls and then a very severe overnight frost the pitch was not only uneven but rock-hard. She'd even wondered whether it was really playable but the ref hadn't said a word about it.

The second half had barely begun when the young man in the red weatherproof jacket, collar turned up, broke into the next verse of his hymn of praise. 'Fantastic tackle, Foggy!

Hope the selectors are watching you. Great stuff!' By now the opposition knew exactly who Foggy was and while their supporters started to jeer him every time he had the ball the Pirates themselves were irritated enough to want to silence his friend. The chance came when Foggy tried to emerge from a mêlée with the ball at his feet. Two boys in blue and yellow sandwiched him and one of them, half-falling at the same time as Foggy went down, levered himself upright again by kneeing Foggy in the thigh. Enraged, Foggy leapt to his feet and launched a wild kick at the boy who'd kneed him.

The fracas couldn't have occurred at a worse place for the referee was practically standing over them.

'Oh no!' Jane exclaimed in despair as she saw the official flourishing the red card. She was too far away to overhear him tell Foggy, who was starting to protest, that if he didn't leave the field without another word, worse would follow. Even Foggy hadn't expected the man to punish his opponent just as severely and Jane was just as surprised but couldn't help experiencing a sense of relief that it wouldn't be ten versus eleven for the rest of the match. By now, of course, the Stonecreek coach was casting baleful glances in her direction, convinced that her earlier chat with the referee had won him over to her side. For, in his opinion, no other ref would have punished them in the same way; everybody else had seen that the Rodale boy was the real aggressor.

Inevitably Foggy was all bluster and threats when he returned to the bench but Jane silenced him immediately. 'Marc, you've been stupid and you've let us down, let us all down. You're out there to play for the team, not to start a personal war! Next game you won't even get on the subs' bench, I can tell you now.'

For a moment he simply looked aghast. Then, grabbing his track suit he stalked off, only to pause and turn after a couple of metres to volley at her, 'Well, if that's how you feel about me, Mrs Allenby, I'm finished with the Kings! I'll find a team that really wants me, one that can see how good I am.'

She made no response apart from moment-arily closing her eyes. If Foggy meant what he said, well, he'd be no great loss in the long run because she could find other players who were at least his equal in skills. Unfortunately, though, she would have to wait until next season to sign a replacement.

'I suspect much of that outburst was really directed at me,' someone said quietly and Jane opened her eyes to find Sam Saxton standing beside her. He was a previous coach of Rodale Goal Kings and many of the present team, including Foggy Thrale, had played for him.

'Oh, Sam, hello, I didn't know you were attending the match. But it's good to see you. What was that about Foggy's outburst?'

'I've been here since the kick-off actually but somewhat disguised under this new hat. My wife persuaded me it was time to swap the old baseball cap for a trilby – more dignified, she says! Anyway, I'm sure Foggy spotted me and that's why we had the performance with his pal chanting his praises.'

'Yes?' Jane prodded, still mystified.

'Oh, sorry, didn't explain, did I? I'm now officially one of the county selectors and also running the rule over any promising lads who might one day fit the bill at national level. Of course, some youngsters feel all they have to do is to put on one really impressive display if I'm around and I'll pick them automatically. Foggy being Foggy calculated that just in case I overlooked him he'd have somebody else draw my attention to his, er, credentials.'

'I see,' replied Jane, who now did. 'Well, it didn't work out as far as I was concerned, did it? So –'

'But you handled it very well, Jane,' Sam cut in. 'He's always been a disruptive element has young Marc and I honestly believe the Kings will be better off without him. You're quite right, players have got to think of the team, not themselves. Seems to me you've got the rest of them doing that, they're playing very well for you. They look a different outfit from the one Ricky Todd gave up on.'

'Oh thank you, Sam, that's very generous of you. However, I don't seem to be getting through to them today. Stonecreek's defence is proving hard to crack.'

Those words were hardly out of her mouth when one of the defenders stumbled while in possession and the ball ran loose. Davey used his electric pace to dart forward to pick it up and then swerve round the centre-back. The Pirates' sweeper, who'd dropped well back simply to speak to his goalie, now charged in to stem the danger and with fine timing won the ball from Davey. The sweeper's newest trick in such circumstances was to spin round through almost a complete circle before parting with the ball. So far it had worked well for him, not least because if carried off to perfection it might tempt an opponent into an offside position. When Davey tried to win the ball back inside the box the sweeper calmly hit the ball sideways to the other side of the area where the left-back was in the perfect position to complete the clearance.

What he'd failed to see was that the ref, always well up with play, was also in the box, and the pass, just fractionally misjudged, hit him instead of the left-back. The official tried to jump out of the way but merely managed to divert the ball to Davey. And Davey, presented with an open goal, wasn't going to miss it.

'Offside!' yelled the Stonecreek defenders and their jack-in-the-box coach. 'Must be!'

The ref, however, waved all protests aside,

though he looked a trifle embarrassed as he did so. The goal counted, the Kings had equalized.

'He's right,' Sam said. 'The ref is like part of the furniture, if the ball hits him it's as if it hit a post. As the Stonecreek player had played the ball last before Davey scored he couldn't be offside. Bit of luck for us, really.'

'Well, we certainly needed it,' agreed Jane, who couldn't help noticing that Sam plainly still regarded the Kings as 'his' team.

'He's turning out to be a good'un is young Davey,' Sam added. 'Didn't impress me very much when I was in charge but you seem to be bringing the best out of him. If he keeps progressing he could go a long way. Not many lads have his acceleration from a standing start. Terrific asset, that.'

Unused to such a flow of compliments from a soccer expert, Jane didn't know what to say but she was delighted Sam approved of Davey's contribution to the team. Though she'd never admit it to anyone, he was probably her favourite player. Moreover, he wasn't nearly as small as most people seemed to think. If he needed to reach a high cross or a corner kick he rarely failed.

The unexpectedness of the goal they'd conceded seemed to affect Stonecreek's confidence and in the final quarter of the match their defence made a string of errors with many players blaming each other audibly for what went wrong. Their coach, who'd long ago decided the ref was really a Kings' supporter in disguise, berated him and his own players in equal measure. Jane was thankful that the ref for once seemed to find no fault with her team since the sending-off incident. She wouldn't have been surprised, though, if he'd officially cautioned her opposite number.

Everyone wearing a watch was looking at it, expecting the final whistle to blow at any second, when the last drama of the match took place. The Kings had been pressing almost continuously since the equalizer but their luck seemed to have run out. Then Larry's persistence on the right won him a corner when he hit the ball against an opponent while trying to get in a cross. Jane didn't need to signal that everyone should move up for it. Already the penalty area was as crowded as a

London tube station at rush-hour.

Tree Forrest produced a gem of an in-swinger, perhaps the best of his life. The goalkeeper, hampered on his line, managed to get a fist to it. But the punch was feeble and the ball simply struck a team-mate on the shoulder – and then ricocheted into the net for an own goal.

'Wow, how lucky can you get!' Jane exclaimed as, seconds later, the ref brought the match to an end. 'I mean, I don't know that we've played well enough to win. But those points are like gold dust!'

'Jane, just remember that in football they all count, the bad goals as well as the good ones,' remarked the former Kings' coach. 'If the luck stays with you, well, who knows what could happen? You could even win the Champion-ship, something I always wanted but never managed.'

8 Title Hopes

Sallie McKinnon put down her coffee cup and smiled at her son on the other side of the breakfast table. 'So,' she enquired, 'how're you feeling on this momentous day?'

'Great,' he replied, though no one would have guessed that from his expression.

'Sure you're not a wee bit nervous? I mean, players who're just about to play in a Cup Final are always supposed to have butterfly flutterings, aren't they? And this is just like a Cup Final for the Kings, you said: the match that can win you the Championship.'

'Well, OK, just a bit nervous,' Frazer admitted. 'Just wish we were playing Scorton Aces 'cos they'll *really* be nervous. I mean, they've finished their programme and they're only a point above us. They've had a terrible run since we thrashed 'em. To be honest, that was what put the skids under 'em.'

Mrs McKinnon, a fanatical card player who adored whist above all games, declared, 'I can see the headline now in the paper – "Kings trump the Aces!" How about that?'

'Very good, Mum,' replied Frazer, impressed. 'Listen, the guys want to get a present for Jane whether we win or not. It's the last game of the season and she's been brilliant. Even took us to Scotland, didn't she? You can't imagine any other coach coming up with a trip like that. But what can we get her? Aye, I know we should've thought of it earlier but we just didn't. Was Davey's idea, actually, his and Danny's.'

'I'm glad you're recognizing the female influence at last,' she said, a trifle smugly. 'Anyway, it's a nice thought so I'll try to come up with some suggestions and pass them on at the end of the match – while you're all celebrating.'

'So who is it you're playing today, then?' enquired Andrea, who came down to breakfast later than the rest of the family.

'Clocklane Strikers. Andi, you *must* have heard us talking about them! The guys who've played for the Kings longest say they're always our *deadliest* rivals. And it's away, too. Listen, you're coming to the match, too, aren't you, with Mum?'

She shrugged, flicking her ponytail to one side. 'Might do. Not much else to do on a Sunday morning if everyone else is out.'

Frazer waited until their mum had left the kitchen before he asked his sister his next question. 'So when we've won the game, *and* the Championship, are you going to give Danny a kiss to celebrate?'

'You must be mad even thinking that!' she retorted and promptly bit into a Danish pastry. Frazer noted, though, that she hadn't said she wouldn't and she definitely turned pink. Then, as he went upstairs to brush his teeth, he started to wonder whether Sophie would turn up, too. According to Danny his would-be girl-friend had said she'd watch him play one day. Sometimes people did keep their promises. If, however, she was no longer really interested in Danny then she might fancy a *Scottish* boyfriend. Frazer had recently decided that his success as a footballer must now be extended to other areas of his life. He would never be a pessimist again.

* * *

'Good luck, darling, you know I'll be thinking of you every minute of the match,' Ken Allenby told his wife as he kissed her goodbye. 'Give me the news on the mobile the moment it's over.'

Jane nodded. 'I will but don't build your hopes up too high. You know I think we've had more than our share of luck in recent weeks. Just hope it doesn't turn against us today of all days.'

'Well, it won't,' Ken insisted. 'That's why I'm staying at home. I haven't seen a game all season and if I change my habit now it'd be sure to change your luck. So remember that my absence is all in your favour!'

'Feeling nervous, Mum?' Dominic asked as they set out for the Clocklane ground in her car. 'I thought I would be but I'm not. I was when we got to the Knock-out Final, though!'

'I suppose I am a bit,' she agreed. 'It seems amazing to me that at the end of a long season full of all sorts of ups and downs everything should depend on the very last match. Because if we don't win everybody – well, nearly everybody – will say the Kings have been a failure. After all, nobody remembers who came second, do they?'

'Don't worry, we *won't* lose. The guys are determined to win it, to win it for *you*. They all think you're the best coach we've ever had. And you are. You're fair to everybody, even Gareth, who's usually the sub, says so! And you got rid of Foggy who was always trouble.'

'Dominic, I think you're being much, *much* too generous. But I really appreciate what you're saying,' Jane smiled at him. A few months ago they'd never have been able to have a chat like this. But the awkwardness between them over team matters had gradually worn away. It still amused her that he addressed her as 'Coach' when they were in the company of his team-mates. Dominic was perfectly content to talk about them and their views although he never disclosed any secrets. He'd implied that the other Kings no longer feared he would carry tales from the dressing-room or that he would get preferential treatment. His own play had improved in the last few matches after he'd gone through a shaky patch following an injury in training.

'Wonder if Foggy or Alex will turn up

today,' Dominic speculated. 'D'you remember it was at Clocklane that Alex got sent off for retaliation? And then his dad rushed on to the pitch to attack the ref, but Alex prevented him from doing it. He actually protected the ref! Crazy!'

'Dominic! The ref *has* to be protected at all times, otherwise the game would descend into chaos. Still, I have to agree: it was one of the few sensible things I saw Alex Todd do. Personally I think Davey's a far better striker than Alex. He's proved it and he's not selfish. I'm really glad for him that he's been picked for the county trial. And Danny. They both thoroughly deserve the honour.'

She half-wished that Dominic, too, had been selected but knew that his mid-season loss of form had probably told against him. Still, if he went on improving at his present rate he could still be called into the county squad for the summer tour.

There was already a buzz going round the trim ground with its distinctive white post-and-rail fence surrounding the pitch. Although there was nothing in this match for the Strikers, who were in mid-table, they were keen to prevent the Kings, fierce rivals for several seasons, from taking the Championship. Jane wasn't surprised to find that even supporters of Scorton Aces were present, inevitably siding with the home fans so that Scorton should win the title.

The chimes that were rung by the Clocklane supporters as a way of lifting their team's spirits were ringing out excitedly as the Strikers ran on to the pitch in their colourful strip of tangerine shirts and yellow shorts. In spite of tempting offers from other teams the previous season, Marcus and Jacko, Clocklane's star players, were still in the side and capable of winning any game on their own. Jane, well aware of their threat, had assigned Josh to look after Jacko whenever the equally tall striker ventured into the box.

'There's really nothing I can say to you now that will make any difference this morning,' Jane told her players in the dressing-room. 'You've been wonderful ever since we came back from that learning exercise in Scotland! You've played the passing game just as I wanted you to. You really deserve to be champions. So, Kings, go out there and show everyone that you really do *rule!*'

'*Yes!*' roared Danny and, bouncing a ball furiously, led the charge out of the building. The Kings were greeted by the loudest applause they'd ever heard for themselves from the biggest crowd of supporters they'd ever seen. Some people had even made their own purple and white flags to wave frantically. Looking round, Jane was surprised by the number of young people present, including several teenage and younger girls. She guessed that most of them were players' sisters rather than girl-friends, although the subject of girl-friends, real or imagined, was rarely mentioned in her hearing. There were also more dads than usual and, not for the first time, Jane wished that her husband was present. Ken Allenby had long hoped that Dominic would become either a boxer or a jockey but, since Dominic had shot up in height and filled out racing horses for a living was out of the question. Ken's strong superstitions, she knew, ruled out any change of habit and so all she could hope was that his absence would, indeed, help to keep their run of luck going.

'You must be thrilled beyond measure at the way things have been going,' Jakki Kelly gushed, ranging up alongside Jane and giving her a very affectionate kiss and hug. 'But you look just as calm as ever. How do you do it, Jane?'

'I'm far from calm inside, believe me!' Jane replied. 'I've always had to look calm, though, haven't I? Delivering babies, I mean. The difference here is that things are literally out of my hands. It's the boys who've got to play and win. All I can do now is encourage them.'

'Well, you've done that all season and that's why the Kings are where they are. That's what all the parents say, Jane. You've proved that a woman can be just as successful as a man at coaching young footballers.'

'Jakki, that's very generous,' murmured Jane, thinking how wonderful it was to receive such praise from a parent and supporter. Too often in junior football it was the mean-spirited and envious who had most to say.

Within five minutes of the kick-off the Goal Kings' coach was convinced their luck had really run out. Cheered on by their enthusiastic fans and their musical chimes, the

Strikers produced some fast, fluid and exciting football. Driven back by the waves of attacks, the Kings' defence conceded successive corners, neither of which was cleared very convincingly by Joe and then Kieren. Only once did a big boot take the ball back to the half-way line and even then it was swiftly returned to Marcus, an attacker whose style was remarkably similar to that of Larry Hill; he too appeared to be all knees and elbows and yet he was hard to dispossess when making a determined run. This time, though, Frazer cleverly took the ball off his toes, looked for someone to pass to when challenged and then, to everyone's amazement, back-heeled the ball to Danny.

But Danny wasn't where Frazer imagined him to be and the ball rolled unstoppably into the empty net. Without any doubt, it was the gaffe of the Kings' season and the gasps around the ground from fans were the loudest sounds until Clocklaners yelled their delight.

'Oh, poor Frazer,' moaned his mum while Andrea took another view.

'Poor goalkeeper, you mean. He never had a chance!'

Jane said nothing because words failed her. She found it almost impossible to believe the evidence of her eyes for Frazer had been one of the successes of the season; he was calm and capable and she couldn't begin to guess what had possessed him to try such a trick in his own box. And, if he had to, why hadn't he called a warning to Danny? 'Use your voice, tell team-mates what's happening': that had been a point she'd hammered time and again in training. Now, in the most crucial game, it'd been forgotten.

'Their nerves've gone, they can't stand the pressure at the top,' a Clocklane supporter exulted. 'We'll walk all over 'em now, you see.'

The Kings' coach couldn't detect any signs of nerves being affected, however. Quite coolly, Frazer took control after a scuffle just outside the box and then weaved his way towards the wing, the ball at his feet. Jane expected some sudden acceleration but instead the Scot dispatched a dream of a pass to Lloyd; and it was Lloyd who made rapid progress after responding to a wall pass from Reuben. Unfortunately Lloyd couldn't get the ball to Davey but at least the Kings had shown a little of their attacking skills.

'*That* was better,' breathed Jakki, who'd stationed herself alongside Jane and was hoping that next season she might officially become assistant coach. 'Shows they haven't lost their confidence.'

'Come on you Clockers, we need another goal,' a fan was yelling as half-time approached. That summed up the match so far because in spite of dominating for so long, the Strikers had failed to score for themselves. Increasingly, the Kings were putting moves together and beginning to look the better side.

All the same, the Kings too were finding it hard to get a shot on target. The nearest they'd come to a goal was a rocket of a shot from Lloyd just inside the box. The ball beat the keeper but not the woodwork, flashing away for a goal-kick after clipping the upright. Even Larry was so impressed he didn't complain that Lloyd should have passed to him instead of shooting. Davey, apparently determined to work harder than ever to mark his selection for the county trials, was tending to drop back to help out in midfield until Jane signalled him to stay upfield. 'That's where you're needed, Davey,' she called. 'Your chance will come.'

It might have been that advice that led to the equalizer. For as soon as Davey moved forward two markers appeared beside him. Then, with perfect timing, Frazer burst down the left and this time kept going all the way to the edge of the box. No one seemed to have any idea of what he would do next, least of all Frazer himself, until he spotted Reuben on the far side of the penalty area, a zone he'd never occupied before as far as any of his team-mates could remember.

'Lefty!' yelled Frazer at the very moment that Reuben's hand went up to demand the ball. Frazer couldn't have flighted it better. Reuben chested it down with ease, swivelled one way before turning the other, and then whipped in a swinging left-foot cross to a point around the penalty spot.

Pulled apart by the changes of direction of the ball the Clocklane defence was wide open as Davey and Larry raced in. But Frazer was there first. After dithering on his line the goalkeeper belatedly rushed out and then, still uncertain, slithered to a halt when he saw he couldn't reach the ball. So he was left helpless as Frazer, on the penalty spot, dropped to his knees and headed the ball into the completely unguarded net.

Naturally Clocklane protested that Frazer was offside but the ref dismissed those claims as 'ridiculous!' Then, after ushering the players back to the centre circle for the resumption he glanced at his stopwatch and promptly blew for the interval.

'Brilliant goal, just brilliant,' Jane told Frazer as the Kings came off the pitch. She also broke one of her own rules by giving him a hug as she did so. It always seemed to her that if she hugged one player in such circumstance she should hug them all; and that was impossible.

'Well, I owed you that one, Coach, after giving the other side *their* goal,' Frazer grinned. 'And, hey, did you know it's my first for the Kings? How about that?'

'Couldn't have come at a better time,' Danny said. 'But next time you're doing a back-pass remember to tell me.'

Oats frowned. 'But I thought you called for it, Dan. *Somebody* did.'

Dominic guessed the answer. 'Typical

Clocklane trick. Must've been one of them. Sure I heard something, too.' Then he remembered something else. 'Hey, Coach, did you see Foggy and Alex? They were sort of *hiding* with those guys from Scorton Aces under the trees at the end we were defending.'

Jane shook her head. 'I've had eyes only for the game, even when people came up and talked to me. Can't say I'm surprised, though. Jealousy is a powerful emotion, you know.'

'Yeah, too right,' Danny murmured mysteriously. Then he immediately cheered up. 'Well, if they stay there they'll see us hit the *winning* goals, won't they, Coach?'

Jane nodded. 'Definitely! Listen, boys, I don't think we need to change much for the second half. You were in command after that sticky start and I'm sure it's only time before we score again. Reuben, you were brilliant in changing the point of attack that led to our equalizer. Try it again sometime but don't overdo it. We want to keep Clocklane guessing about what we'll do next. So, keep ruling, Kings!'

Exactly what instructions the Strikers had been given Jane didn't know but she could guess for they attacked from the kick-off with unrelenting fury. Marcus was like a player possessed, darting, driving, charging, barging just about everywhere. One moment he was brought down by Dominic right on the edge of the box (but failed to gain a penalty in spite of wholesale protests from the team); and the next moment he picked up a booking for elbowing Josh out of the way. In the ceaseless attacks Josh's height was invaluable for he never missed a heading chance and he twice intercepted crosses at full-stretch to foil the towering Jacko. Curiously enough, Danny didn't really have much handling to do because his co-defenders were in such resilient form.

The home side's supporters were shouting themselves hoarse and so, orchestrated by the bells-ringer, the noise swelling around the ground was awesome. 'You'd think this was a Cup Final between local rivals, wouldn't you?' Jakki yelled into Jane's ear. Jane nodded. 'It is *our* Cup Final in a way. If we don't win it we lose all we've worked for this season.'

She'd never thought of it in quite those terms and now she remembered Foggy and

Alex. They were just visible with the Scorton fans and she wondered how they were feeling. After all, they wouldn't get anything out of the season. Still, it was hard to feel sympathy for them because they'd cared only for themselves, never for the team. There was no sign of Ricky Todd or Sam Saxton but then she hadn't expected them to be here. Whatever the outcome of this match, she was going to invite both her predecessors to the Kings' end-of-season party.

It took a long throw from Danny to Frazer to relieve the siege conditions and, once again, the Scot flew down the flank at a pace that astonished some spectators and his nearest opponents. This time he wasn't able to find Reuben in quite such a good position for a cross. Still, Larry was available for a pass and when he launched one of his charges it took a crunching tackle to bring it to a premature end. In spite of the very physical nature of the game it was the first time Jane had been needed on the pitch in her role as physio. Larry, however, waved her away even while still vigorously rubbing his calf. 'I'm fine, Coach, it'll wear off,' he assured her. At that moment Jane sensed that they were going to do it; the spirit in the team wouldn't allow for anything else.

The free kick came to nothing even though Tree Forrest flung himself headlong at the ball in a vain effort to head it just inside the post. His speed to return to his defensive position was impressive for someone regarded as the slowest mover in the squad.

That attack seemed to be pivotal in the fortunes of the game for after that Clocklane's fizz died away; and the Kings regained the initiative they'd held at the end of the first half before Frazer levelled the scores. Reuben, revelling in his role of wandering playmaker with a licence to strike for goal, was at pains to keep possession for as long as possible. Lloyd, darting from one flank to the other, was the perfect foil and it was clear to every spectator that the Clocklane defence didn't really know how to deal with them. On the other hand, the Kings couldn't get the goal they needed. Without that goal, the Championship would go to Scorton.

'Just one little bit of luck, that's all we need,' Jane pleaded. She knew that large slices of it had come their way this season but surely no one could begrudge them just one more grain. She glanced at her watch for the thousandth time and calculated that two minutes were all that remained to them of the Highlea Junior Sunday League season.

Then another attack, inspired again by Frazer, developed down the left. When the ball reached him Davey audaciously chipped it across to Reuben on the corner of the box. Reuben pulled it down, spun through almost a complete circle – and was brought down by a panicking, blundering defender.

'Penalty!' yelled every Kings' supporter.

'*No!*' roared the Clocklane fans and players.

The referee, who'd been close to the incident, deliberated for some moments while the fevers of hope and despair swirled around him. And then, very firmly, he pointed to the spot. '*Yes!*' chorused the Kings. And the Clocklane contingent fell silent.

Davey collected the ball, rubbed away any microscopic amount of earth or grass adhering to it, and then placed it on the penalty spot. Jane could think of only one thing, that her prayers really had been answered for she didn't believe the foul on Reuben had been inside the area. So would their luck go the other way now, at the eleventh hour and fifty-ninth minute?

Davey's run was short, his shot powerfully struck, and he sent the goalie the wrong way. But, astonishingly, the ball flicked against the goalie's left boot and from there shot high into the air. Inevitably, Davey was the first player to react: his speed got him to the hanging ball first and he hardly needed to jump to head it into the net for the goal that clinched the Championship for Rodale Goal Kings.

There was just time for the kick-off again but nothing more. So the pitch invasion that had started with the goal and then been stopped by the ref's threats to abandon the match now went ahead without interruption. Jane found herself swept up by the euphoria of fans and players and parents alike and as far as she was concerned this kind of excitement could go on for ever. She knew she'd never get tired of it.

As the players leapt about and hugged everyone in reach Frazer saw Andrea dash across the pitch to give Danny a kiss; but she didn't stop with him because before he could say a word to her she was running away again to kiss Reuben, who looked as pleased as he was surprised. She might have stayed with him but suddenly Danny, as skipper, was gathering all his team-mates together along with Jane. With the remaining Clocklane players and supporters now leaving the pitch the victorious team occupied the centre circle.

And there, in one voice, they sang and sang, 'Goal Kings rule, Goal Kings rule, Goal Kings rule!'

No one present could possibly doubt it.

If you particularly enjoy reading about football, why not try some of these other Faber children's books?

Goal Kings by Michael Hardcastle

BOOK ONE: Shoot-Out
BOOK TWO: Eye For A Goal
BOOK THREE: And Davey Must Score
BOOK FOUR: They All Count

Life in the Junior Football League can be tough. This adventure-packed series follows the dramas and excitements – on and off the pitch – in the lives of Goal Kings JFC.

Own Goal by Michael Hardcastle

Russell is passionate about football but he has a problem: he scores own goals. Then, amazingly, he discovers a footballing talent he never dared dream of.

One Kick by Michael Hardcastle

Jamie finds that all is not fair play on the

field, and makes a mistake that is to haunt him for weeks and almost put a stop to his footballing career . . .

Second Chance by Michael Hardcastle

Scott is an ace striker. But when he moves to a school where soccer comes a poor second to cricket, he faces an unexpected and difficult challenge . . .

Frances Fairweather: Demon Striker!
by Derek Smith

Frances is so obsessed with football that she gets thrown out of the girls' team, and the boys' team won't have her either. Drastic measures are called for: Frances decides to become 'Frank' . . .

Faber children's books are available from bookshops. For a complete catalogue, please write to: The Children's Marketing Department, Faber and Faber, 3 Queen Square, London WC1N 3AU.